THE BISHOP'S PALACE

Elizabeth Parker comes to Brazil to take up a job as a schoolteacher in the declining city of Manalos, skirting the Amazonian jungle. Hoping to start a new life, she instead finds forbidden love with the husband of her employer, the aristocratic Kitty Drayton, who lives in a decaying mansion with her spinster sister. The atmosphere of unease surrounding Elizabeth steadily grows into terror as she is stalked by a sinister figure during Rio's Carnival, culminating in a shocking murder — for which she becomes the obvious suspect . . .

V. J. BANIS

THE BISHOP'S PALACE

Complete and Unabridged

LINFORD
Leicester

First published in Great Britain

First Linford Edition
published 2015

A catalogue record for this book is available
from the British Library.

ISBN 978–1–4448–2554–1

Published by
F. A. Thorpe (Publishing)
Anstey, Leicestershire

Set by Words & Graphics Ltd.
Anstey, Leicestershire
Printed and bound in Great Britain by
T. J. International Ltd., Padstow, Cornwall

This book is printed on acid-free paper

1

The knocking at the door was loud and insistent. Elizabeth Parker answered the summons and found two gentlemen there, one in the uniform of the local police and the other in a rather crumpled suit.

'Senhorita Parker?' the man in the suit asked. Elizabeth nodded, her throat so dry she did not trust her voice to speak. Her first thought was of Karl — something had happened to Karl.

'I am Senhor Mendoza of the Manalos civil police,' he introduced himself, 'and this is Captain Lopez. May we come in?'

She opened the door wider and they stepped in, closing the door after themselves. 'Is something wrong?' she asked. 'Has something happened?'

Lopez took up a position by the door and remained silent. Mendoza, who seemed to be in charge, ignored her question and said instead, 'You arrived back in Manalos yesterday, Senhorita, that is correct?'

'Yes, that is correct, but — '

He gave her no chance to speak but went on smoothly. While he spoke, his eyes continued to look around and around the room, as if searching for something, but she had no idea what it might be. 'You have been here, in the hotel, most of the time since your return, is that right?' She nodded, growing increasingly impatient for him to explain. 'And last night, you were visited by Senhora Drayton, were you not?'

Elizabeth stiffened. Something cold touched the base of her spine, like an icy finger. 'She was here briefly, yes. Not here in my room, but downstairs. She came by my table while I was eating dinner.'

'You had a quarrel, I understand.' For the first time he turned his dark eyes, cold and penetrating, directly upon her. 'A quarrel over Mr. Drayton who, if I understand correctly, planned to leave Manalos and his wife and go away with you.'

'I'm not sure that's anyone's business,' Elizabeth said sharply. Her mind was racing, trying to think where all this could be leading. She had forgotten she was in an almost forgotten city deep in the Amazon rainforest, and that in this city Kitty Drayton was a powerful political force. She did not know what limits the law put on personal vengeance, but it was entirely possible that in some way Kitty meant to use the law against her. Perhaps she even meant to have her arrested on some trumped-up charge. It occurred to her that she did not know the local law at all.

Senhor Mendoza ignored her remark. 'Senhora Drayton told you, I believe, that the only way you could leave with Senhor Drayton was over her dead body. That is the phrase she used, is it not?'

'You seem very well informed already,' Elizabeth said coldly. 'But, yes, a number of people overheard our quarrel. It was only a figure of speech, as I'm sure you must know.'

Senhor Mendoza said, 'Ah, but in this instance it has proved to be more than just a figure of speech, would it not seem?'

Elizabeth looked at him blankly. 'I don't understand what you mean,' she said.

He smiled without a trace of cheer. 'Senhora Drayton told you *how* you could have her husband, and now it has been arranged, just as she suggested.'

For a moment Elizabeth still could not comprehend what he was trying to tell her. 'I don't . . . ' she stammered.

'Or did you not know? Senhora Drayton is dead.'

Elizabeth took a step backward and one hand went to her throat. 'Kitty? Dead? But, how? She was fine yesterday.'

'Yes, so I am told,' Senhor Mendoza replied. 'As to how, she has been murdered. Poisoned.'

The simple word, delivered in a soft, unemotional voice, was like the explosion of a bomb in the little hotel room.

'I — I must sit down,' Elizabeth said, feeling dazed.

The policeman was at once all sympathy, leaping to her side and guiding her toward one of the chairs near the window.

'Sit,' he said, and to the uniformed Lopez, 'Bring her some water, quickly.'

He held the glass for her while she took a long drink. He did not seem threatening now, but rather kind and gentle. Still, even in her dazed state, she could not help seeing the significance of his visit here.

'You said — ' She stumbled over the word. ' — murdered. Poisoned. But surely that can't be . . . '

Through the window she could just see the sunlight glinting off the water of the Rio Negro. Was it really no more than a few months ago that she had first travelled down that river? She and Kitty, with nothing between them but the beginnings of a friendship — or so she had thought. If she'd only had some idea where she was going, what was ahead for her. But who could ever know what the future held for them, for good . . . or for evil?

Captain Mendoza cleared his throat. Of course, she thought, they believed she had murdered Kitty. She could see how it must look to them. How could she make them see, make them understand that she and Kitty had started off as friends? At least, in Kitty's mind. Kitty had proclaimed their friendship so often and so loudly, and she — Elizabeth — had tried to make it so.

But friendship had turned to enmity — deadly enmity, it seemed now; certainly deadly for Kitty. And for her as well, unless she could convince them of her innocence.

And it had been innocent back then, on the boat, on the river. At the beginning.

How blind she had been, blind and foolish . . .

* * *

'Let me tell you,' the woman on the boat told Elizabeth Parker, 'the first time you wake up and find a snake in your bed, you'll wish you were home.'

Elizabeth thought, *I wish I were home already. But I have no home.*

They were standing at the railing of a boat, the *Fair Lady*. The brown water of the Amazon River flowed below. The distant shore was lush and green, flecked with bright bits of scarlet and lavender and pink that were probably some sort of tropical blossom but from this distance appeared only as scattered bits of confetti.

'I'm going up to Manalos,' Elizabeth said. 'I've heard it's a charming city.'

The woman beside her threw back her head and laughed heartily. 'Charming? Forty or fifty years ago I suppose it was.'

'But I was told Manalos was a very nice city. Very cultured, with an opera house and several fine hotels, and . . . '

'A long time ago,' her companion said, 'at one time, Manalos and Manaus were twin boom towns. Brazil is full of them. Have you ever heard of Ouro Preto? It was a gold town at one time, and they used to call Diamantina, the diamond center of the world. I'll bet you've never heard of either of them, have you? Well, Manaus and Manalos were rubber towns and at one time they must have been quite the cultural centers — all those rubber barons with more money than they could spend. But it didn't last.'

'What happened?'

'The plantations in Malaya and the

Dutch East Indies started to out-produce and undersell Brazil. When the synthetics came along the boom towns became ghost towns. Manaus was the better known, but Manalos was the grandest of the boom towns once. Those days are long since past. It's a crumbling graveyard now.' Her eyes narrowed shrewdly. 'Say, did some man tell you that nonsense, to get you to come here?'

Elizabeth smiled at the implication. She had long since grown accustomed to thinking of herself as plain. She had no outstanding features other than her eyes, and they were so large and dark in contrast to her pale skin that her father had always said she looked like a frightened doe. She had hair of an ashy blonde color, which she kept primly pulled back from her face, and for this trip upriver she had worn a simple cotton blouse and a denim skirt. She was hardly the sort to cause men to spin such elaborate webs of seduction.

'Actually,' she said, 'I was given a job in Manalos, as a schoolteacher.'

'Were you hired by Kitty Drayton?' the

woman asked guardedly.

'As a matter of fact I was,' Elizabeth said, surprised. 'Do you know her?'

'Everyone in this part of the world knows her. Are you an old friend of Kitty's?'

'I only met her when she interviewed me for the job.'

Her companion seemed to relax a bit. 'Have you got a place to stay in Manalos?'

'Mrs. Drayton arranged rooms for me at a hotel until I find something to my liking.'

'I doubt that you ever will in Manalos. But I have a room I sometimes rent out. You might be comfortable in it. It's nothing fancy, but it's a lot nicer than the hotel, I promise you. Why don't you come look at it when you get in and see what you think? My name is Edwards, Ruth Edwards. My husband has a store in town, a sort of general emporium — which is why I stay, if you've wondered.'

'I'm Elizabeth Parker. I'm pleased to meet you.'

She was pleased, too. Although she would never have shown it, she could not help but be frightened by this journey she was taking. She had never traveled to speak of, and this was such a long trip. It was some comfort to have at least one friend at her destination.

'If you don't mind my saying so, there are a lot of places that I would think would be more suitable for a young lady like yourself than Manalos.'

'I don't mind your saying so,' Elizabeth laughed. 'But to be frank, none of them offered me a job, and Mrs. Drayton did. I don't have a degree, you see, which is a problem in the States, but Mrs. Drayton seemed to think she could make that all right with the school board in Manalos, and . . . '

'She owns the school board, so I don't think you have to worry about that. Well, there, I didn't mean to spoil the trip for you. I'd better look now and see if they've got my cabin anywhere near right. Mind you look your bed over carefully at night before you get into it.' With that ominous piece of advice, Mrs. Edwards took her leave.

Elizabeth remained at the rail, gazing at

the green in the distance. This other-worldly river with its jungle shore was now her world. She could see nothing anywhere but the brown water and the green forests and this boat moving through them. Since they had left Belem some time earlier, she had seen no sign of life but an occasional cluster of huts along the river, unoccupied for all she could tell. Somewhere beyond these jungles lay Manalos. And behind her . . .

The past was no haven of fond memories, but even in the bitterest times there had been a few moments of brightness, occasioned chiefly by her father. How she had adored him. It was inevitable, no doubt, being raised by him as she had been after her mother's death. Their lives had kept them so occupied that there had been no close ties with other adults, and aside from her father nearly all the friendships she'd had over the past ten years had been with children. Unattached children, as her father would have put it.

So when he began their little enterprise, it had not been an orphanage but the

Parker Home for Unattached Children. And in starting it, he had grossly overestimated their slim capabilities, or underestimated what it would take for such a project. It had devoured his savings greedily, and all their time and their energies. She had taught the younger children, and cooked, and he had done nearly everything else.

'Eventually,' he insisted all the while, 'we'll be able to hire some help.' That 'eventually,' however, had never come.

Her eyes misted and the river scene before her faded. In her mind's eye she saw her father as he had been in those ten years. Of course, she did an injustice to think of those years as nothing but bitterness and work and hardship. For all it had taken from them, the home had given them so much in return — a harvest of love and goodness. Mostly it had been through his efforts, but she had been happy and proud to help.

It all ended so very suddenly, in a fire that destroyed virtually everything. None of the children were harmed, and for that they thanked God over and over; but the home had gone completely, and every non-living thing in it, and the insurance money was just too little to enable them to start again. Indeed, there had been a positive wealth of debts that seemed endless. The children had to be placed elsewhere, in local orphanages. The dream was dead. It had to be buried.

Her father had died just a few months later. 'Natural causes,' the doctor had said. Perhaps. If heartbreak was considered a 'natural cause.'

She was left with nothing but a tiny furnished apartment with enough money on hand to see her through maybe two months, if she were really careful. She had no family and no friends who were older than eleven years. She was qualified to do very little that could earn her a living, and hadn't the credentials to teach in a public school.

At this critical moment Kitty Drayton had appeared, looking for a school-teacher. Someone who needn't have teaching credentials per se, depending upon her experience, but she must be free to travel to South America, to a city called Manalos, in the Amazon jungle.

'Right now,' Elizabeth had said when the phone call had come, 'I'd travel to hell and back if I had to for a job.'

'And here I am,' she said aloud, coming back to the present moment.

'Yes, here you are,' Mrs. Drayton's high, rather self-consciously musical voice said from behind her.

Elizabeth turned. 'Hello,' she said, 'I didn't hear you.'

'My husband Karl says I move on little cat's feet,' Mrs. Drayton said with a dazzling smile. 'Isn't that poetic? You looked like you were daydreaming.'

'I was.' Elizabeth had tried to warm to Mrs. Drayton's efforts to be friendly but it was difficult. She was pretty in a delicate, almost child-like way, with white skin that seemed never to have been touched by a sunbeam and glossy black hair. Elizabeth found her too sweet, too gay, the smile too dazzling and too ready.

Perhaps she was being unjust. There was something actually sad about this too-bright woman. Kitty Drayton seemed so determined to be happy that you couldn't help thinking she must be sad.

She could not recall how many times Mrs. Drayton had insisted, 'We're going to be the best of friends.'

Mrs. Drayton was forty-five. It had come as a shock to Elizabeth to learn this because at a glance she had taken her to be twenty-five at the most. It was not only that she looked young and dressed young — she acted young. Her voice was high and girlish, her gestures those of a coquette. She had exactly the manner of a young girl on her first trip alone.

'Well, we can't have you looking like you were already homesick,' Mrs. Drayton said now. 'You come along with me and I'll introduce you to my husband.'

They went up the stairs to what Mrs. Drayton informed her was the hurricane deck. There was a long, narrow cabin above that. 'That's where the officers have their quarters,' she told Elizabeth, 'and that's the pilothouse above it. We'll go up.'

A sign at the foot of the stairs said plainly, 'No passengers permitted beyond this point.' Elizabeth made a gesture in the direction of the sign. 'Do you think we should?'

'Heavens, why on earth not?' Mrs. Drayton laughed, but Elizabeth thought she did not sound entirely sure of herself. She clutched Elizabeth's arm with her long, elegant fingers. 'We're going to be the best of friends, I just know it,' she said, 'and I'm going to start by calling you Liz. Is that all right?'

'If you like,' said Elizabeth, who had never been anything less than Elizabeth.

Elizabeth had met the boat's Captain Warren on the day Mrs. Drayton interviewed her for the job. She remembered him as a tall, thin man, fifty-ish, with a ready smile, who seemed very sure of himself. Oddly, though Elizabeth had found him easy to like, she saw at once that Mrs. Drayton was not comfortable in his presence.

'Captain Warren is an awful flatterer, you know,' she chirped after he left. 'You mustn't take anything he says seriously.' Elizabeth hadn't taken him seriously, in fact, but she wondered that Kitty thought it necessary to say so.

It was apparent as they approached the pilot house that Captain Warren was berating his cabin boy, a native in a white coat who looked apologetic and upset. Elizabeth would have thought it more tactful not to interrupt, but when they reached the top step Mrs. Drayton turned the doorknob without pausing. When the door did not open, she rattled it for attention.

At once the cabin boy came over to open it, and when the women stepped inside he flew out and down the stairs, obviously grateful for the opportunity to escape.

'I'm afraid your husband isn't here just now,' the captain said, his face noncommittal. 'We had a little problem with a boiler. He's below seeing to that.'

'Oh well, never mind,' Mrs. Drayton said gaily. 'I've brought Miss Parker up to see the pilothouse, not my husband.'

Elizabeth felt they ought not to have come up, but Captain Warren kept his face impassive while Mrs. Drayton moved around the pilothouse. She had relinquished her hold on Elizabeth's arm and was busy explaining the big pilot wheel and the braided bell cords used to signal

17

the engineer below.

'It's a very old-fashioned boat,' she said.

'The *Fair Lady* is a direct descendant of your American riverboats,' the captain said with a note of pride and affection in his voice.

'I'm afraid ours are pretty much a thing of the past,' Elizabeth said. 'One or two of them still go up and down the Mississippi as pleasure boats.'

There came the sound of footsteps on the stairs. Elizabeth turned as a tall man of thirty or so came in. 'It's fixed now,' he said before he saw the two women. 'But it was like an inferno down there.'

His white shirt and white trousers were drenched with sweat and clung to his body. Elizabeth looked away, blushing.

'Sorry,' he said, his expression blank, 'I've been down in the boiler room.' He wiped some sweat from his brow and leaned over to take his jacket off a hook on the wall. He slapped a cap on his head and turned back to them.

There was an awkward silence. Kitty Drayton looked embarrassed and even guilty. 'Oh Karl, darling,' she said, 'I was just showing Miss Parker the boat. She's our new schoolteacher, and I just know she and I are going to be the best of friends. Liz, honey, this is my husband, Karl Drayton. Captain Drayton, I should say.'

Elizabeth had already surmised who he must be and had gotten over the surprise of discovering that he was easily ten years his wife's junior. He was not really handsome. His face was rather broad over high cheekbones, his mouth wide and sensuous. He stood quite still and his piercing blue eyes regarded Elizabeth with an almost frightening intensity. She had the impression that his self-control was only a net of delicate threads that held in uneasy check a wild and savage nature.

'How do you do,' she said aloud, embarrassed both by her instinctive reaction to his physicality and by the situation in which she had been placed. It seemed, to her at least, that Mr. Drayton was not pleased to find them here. 'It's a very lovely boat. We were just leaving.'

She moved toward the door. He smiled and she was rather more surprised by that than she had been by his age — which on reflection, did not seem so very important. Kitty Drayton was hardly more than a child, and she had heard men liked that in a woman.

He said, with an utter lack of conviction, 'I'm pleased to meet you.'

'Thank you. I'm sure you gentlemen must be busy.' Elizabeth tried the door but it had stuck, to her further embarrassment. She had to look around at Captain Warren, who at once jumped to her side and opened it for her.

Mrs. Drayton, meanwhile, their exit delayed, had launched upon an animated monologue directed at her husband and concerned primarily with her 'little girl.' Since he did not encourage her by answering, she tossed phrases over her shoulder in Elizabeth's direction without waiting for replies to any of them.

'I found the most darling pink outfit for her,' she prattled. 'Liz, you'll just love my little Caroline; she's the prettiest child I've ever laid eyes upon. Karl, sweetheart,

I hope you won't scold me; I did spend a lot of money, but you do want your ladies to look pretty, don't you?'

When she paused for breath, he said flatly, 'It is your money.'

Even she had no answer for that. Another silence fell. Elizabeth stood at the open door, her back to them, looking out over the railing. Since they'd been inside, the jungle had moved closer to the side of the ship. A monkey swung high on a bough and macaws and parrots hovered nearby. The brown river water turned yellow in the reflection of the sinking sun. The evening air smelled dank and sweetly rotten.

Mrs. Drayton said brightly, 'Well, we'll see you at dinner. We have to hurry along now. You've kept us here too long as it is, and I don't fool myself that it was because of *my* charms, you naughty boys.'

She followed Elizabeth down the stairs. Elizabeth was angry with her for having taken them up there in the first place. When she happened to glance back, however, she saw Mrs. Drayton biting her trembling lip and staring off toward the setting sun. Elizabeth's anger melted. She could not help feeling sorry for her, as she would have felt sorry for a child who had done something that was forbidden and had been punished for it rather more severely than was warranted.

'Isn't my Karl the handsomest man you've ever seen?' Mrs. Drayton said.

'Is he?' Elizabeth said. 'Yes, I suppose he is good-looking. I hadn't really thought about it.' To change the subject, she asked, 'Why does the boat have two captains?'

'Oh, Karl isn't on the boat as captain. He's the owner. That is, we own the lines. Captain Warren is in charge, actually. Karl just came along — well, if you want the truth, I think he just meant to keep an eye on me. He treats me just like his little girl, but I can't say I mind. It's always been like that for me. I was my father's darling, too, and Walter — that was my first husband — you'd have thought I just came down from Heaven to pay him a visit.'

They went to the guardrail together and watched the river for a time. It looked as if they and the boat were motionless and the shore were moving slowly along past them. It gave Elizabeth a queer feeling, as if her world were slipping away.

As they stood there the throb of the engines ceased. The boat slowed and then stopped. 'We're anchoring at the entrance to the Narrows,' Kitty explained. 'Manalos sits on the bank of the Rio Negro, but we have to wait for daybreak before we dare pass through to the tiny channel that takes us there.'

Elizabeth suddenly wanted to be done with the boat. She felt stifled on it, and wanted the feel of solid earth beneath her feet.

As if sensing her thoughts, Kitty said, 'It means we'll have a nice, quiet night to sleep. Those engines are the noisiest things in Christendom, don't you agree?'

The sun set and as suddenly as if a curtain had fallen, it was dusk; time to go below for dinner. Elizabeth thought the sunset on the river was beautiful and she would have preferred to remain on deck to watch it to its conclusion, but she did not want to abandon Mrs. Drayton, who still looked a bit anxious.

Karl Drayton did not join them for dinner. Mrs. Drayton said she was disappointed.

2

In her cabin, Elizabeth remembered Mrs. Edwards's admonition to check her bed carefully. She found nothing there, but as she was undressing an enormous cockroach skittered across the ceiling and disappeared into a crack in the wood paneling.

She stretched out on the narrow bed. She could just glimpse the deck rail through the tiny window and watch the shadows play upon it.

Now that it was at rest, a deep silence enveloped the clumsy boat. A bird called in the distance, and the silence closed in again. She could not help wondering what new world, what strange way of life, awaited her at her destination.

An image of Karl Drayton came uninvited into her mind. So tall and well sculptured, surrounded as he was by an almost visible aura of masculinity.

'I mustn't think such thoughts,' she

scolded herself. She closed her eyes, making herself breathe deeply, and soon was fast asleep.

Ever so subtly her subconscious was aware that someone was standing over her, looking down at her, bringing her gradually awake. She felt an ominous chill. She knew someone was in her cabin, but she could not imagine who or why. Nor could she bring herself to open her eyes, but continued instead to pretend to sleep.

A door creaked. At once her eyes flew open and she was on her feet, crossing the tiny cabin to the door. She opened it stealthily and peered out. She had a glimpse of someone disappearing around a corner, someone in a fluffy pink nightgown that she had admired only a short while before as she watched Kitty Drayton unpack her things in her own cabin.

Elizabeth closed the door of her cabin and this time remembered to lock it. Why, she wondered, returning to her bed, should Kitty Drayton have come to her room in the night, while she slept?

* * *

It was barely dawn when she woke again. Remembering the damp, oppressive heat of the previous day, she thought it would be pleasant to take advantage of this cooler hour and she dressed quickly, making her way out to the deck.

To her surprise the boat was already moving again, and when she came out she saw that they were into the narrow channel that would take them to the mainstream of the Rio Negro. The surrounding trees were so close that they almost brushed the ship on either side. She felt stifled by the closeness of the vegetation.

A sudden shriek, like a scream, startled her.

'That was a jaguar.'

She started again and turned to find Captain Drayton standing close behind her. 'Good morning,' she said, and looked back to the jungle. 'Are they common?'

'Very. The road that goes from Belem to Brasilia is called the Jaguar's Promenade. You're up early. Wasn't your stateroom comfortable?'

'Quite comfortable, thank you. I just supposed it would be cooler this early.'

'Yes, the heat takes some getting used to.'

He had come to stand at the rail beside her. He seemed to her much as he had the day before, civil, but with a forced civility. 'This will clear away soon,' he said, indicating a tendril of river mist that floated up toward them.

'I've never seen the jungle before,' she said.

'And do you think you'll like it?'

'It's a little early to say,' she answered evasively. She smiled up at him. 'Please, you don't have to stand here making conversation with me. You were perfectly right to be annoyed when you found me in the pilot house yesterday. Your sign was most explicit.'

'Do you think I am trying to apologize now?'

'I've no idea, but Mrs. Drayton did say yesterday that a captain is condemned to be polite to his passengers.'

Abruptly he changed the subject. 'Did

you know my wife before she interviewed you for your job?'

'No, not at all.' She thought he and his wife must not be very closely acquainted if he had to ask her that.

'And do your relatives not mind your going off into the mysterious jungle like this?'

'I have no relatives. My father recently passed away. I'm afraid I'm quite on my own.'

'I'm sorry to hear that.' After a moment he asked, 'And has no one talked of me?'

'Your wife talks of you often, and quite flatteringly.'

He smiled at her remark but said nothing. For a time they watched in silence as the jungle inched by.

Unexpectedly, he said, 'You're a fine young woman.'

She smiled and said in a teasing voice, 'I suppose being a captain, you have the authority to make such quick judgments.'

He returned her smile and she was surprised by how it transformed his rather solemn face. How could she ever have thought he wasn't handsome?

The cabin boy from the previous day's misadventure came up from below carrying a coffeepot on a tray, and with no more than a glance in their direction, continued up toward the pilot house. The aroma of freshly brewed coffee came and went with him.

'I think I'll have my breakfast now,' she said.

'If there is anything I can do to make your trip more pleasant, please let me know,' Captain Drayton said. He gave a little bow and went up the steps in the wake of the cabin boy.

Elizabeth stared after him, unnerved by the odd quickening of her senses that he had stirred in her. She turned toward the stairs that led downward and was surprised to see Kitty Drayton standing there, watching her. For a fraction of a second, no more than that, she thought she saw something ugly and violent in Kitty's expression — a look directed at her of pure, venomous hatred.

It was gone quickly, replaced by Kitty's syrupy smile. Elizabeth was sure she must have imagined that other emotion.

'There you are,' Kitty said, coming toward her with arms outstretched. 'I've been hunting all over for you, to have breakfast.'

They came down together to the dining room.

'Did you have trouble sleeping?' Elizabeth asked while they were being served.

'Oh dear no, I always sleep like a dead man on these boats. The motion of the boat on the water rocks me right to sleep. No, I left you and had a cup of tea in my cabin and was asleep within ten minutes.'

Puzzled, Elizabeth asked, 'Weren't you up during the night?'

'Not I. What makes you ask that?'

'I — I thought I saw you in the corridor.'

'Perhaps you just dreamed it. Oh, doesn't everything look delicious?'

A white-jacketed waiter served them an elaborate breakfast from a rolling cart, as well as milk and plenty of hot coffee.

Mrs. Drayton took an egg and a biscuit but hardly touched either. She put a dollop of strawberry jam on her plate and nibbled at that with a spoon until she had finished it. She gave a surreptitious glance around, as if looking to see if anyone were watching her, and took another spoonful of the jam.

'I'm not allowed to do this at home,' she said, nibbling. 'Amelie wouldn't let me. She's our housekeeper, and she's wonderful with my little angel; but honestly, she treats me like I was the same age as Caroline. Of course, she's been with us since I was a baby. The Deodoras — I'm a Deodora, before I was married — have always had black servants. It used to be slaves, but now of course they're just hired help.'

She managed to make their unwillingness to continue as slaves sound like an injustice on the part of the blacks. Elizabeth, eating a selection of the foods from the trays, did not reply.

'What were you and Captain Drayton talking about this morning?' Kitty asked out of the blue, nibbling.

Elizabeth looked up and found those bright dark eyes fastened on her. Innocent though her conversation with the captain had been, Elizabeth felt guilty nonetheless.

'Nothing in particular that I recall,' she said.

'You looked so very involved with your conversation.'

Elizabeth shrugged. 'We talked about jaguars and the jungle. Is it so very important?'

'No, of course not,' Kitty said, finishing off the strawberry jam. 'I told him he was very rude to you yesterday and that he should be more agreeable. Was he?'

'Very agreeable,' Elizabeth said. For some reason she blushed when she said that and found it necessary to look down at her plate.

* * *

Elizabeth's first impression of Manalos was that the city was floating. She had a view of thatched roofs bobbing up and down in the river current, and it was a moment or so before she realized that these were the roofs of raft-houses that lined the riverbank.

'Some of these people ply the river as tradesmen,' Mrs. Edwards said beside

33

her. Elizabeth had, after further discussion, decided that she would accept the offer of a room to let, as it sounded a little more pleasant than a hotel room.

'Is there much commerce?' Elizabeth asked.

'No. These river highways ought to be important, as they are in other countries, but they aren't. Some tropical produce, the pickings of the hunters, that's about it.'

Kitty Drayton appeared beside them, exchanging lukewarm greetings with Mrs. Edwards. To Elizabeth she said, 'I'm just going up to say goodbye to my husband. You must come with me.'

'I should think you would rather be alone for a few minutes.'

'Don't be silly,' Kitty insisted. 'I want you to come. We won't embarrass you. We're an old married couple, you know. We'll say goodbye and he'll give me a peck on the cheek, that's all. Come along.'

They met Captain Drayton on the stairs, coming down from the pilot house. 'I was just coming to see that you got off all right,' he said. 'It's only a brief pause.'

'Doesn't the boat stop at Manalos?' Elizabeth asked.

'Not to stay,' he said. 'Not yet, anyway. There are some settlements further upriver that we go to before we turn around and come back, but there's no reason for you to ride all that way.'

'I don't see why you have to ride all that way either,' Kitty said in a peevish tone. 'I mean, after all, you aren't really needed on board. Captain Warren is here to run the boat.'

'It's important that I make these runs,' he said in the voice of a man who was repeating something he had said many times before.

The boat slowed and bumped against the wharf. Kitty looked around. 'Well, I'll say goodbye now. I brought Liz up because she's afraid of you.'

Elizabeth blushed and said, 'No, I've had a lovely trip. Thank you for everything.' She was even more embarrassed to see, from the brief look he gave her, that Captain Drayton understood her embarrassment. It seemed to put the captain and her on a strange level of intimacy that his wife could not share, which gave Elizabeth rather a queer sensation.

Kitty stood on tiptoe, putting her hands on her husband's shoulders, and kissed his cheek lightly. Elizabeth looked away. When she looked at them again, she was astonished to see that even as he kissed his wife, Captain Drayton was staring past Kitty directly at her. She looked quickly away again and waited until Kitty said, 'There now, don't make a complete mess of my makeup.'

'Goodbye, Miss Parker,' Captain Drayton said. 'It's been a pleasure having you on board. I hope you enjoy Manalos.'

'I know that she will,' Kitty said. 'We're going to be the best of friends.'

As they were going toward the ramp, Kitty asked, 'Do you believe in love at first sight?'

'I've never given it much thought.'

'I do. That's how I fell in love with Captain Drayton.'

Elizabeth made no answer to that.

On the dock she parted with Mrs. Drayton and went instead with Mrs. Edwards. It was a Saturday and a surprising number of people had come down to see the boat come in. This was, apparently, something of a treat, and there was the air of a fiesta. Families and friends exchanged greetings. One small boy tried to sell Elizabeth American-style cigarettes and another insisted that he must polish her shoes for her.

Beyond the landing lay a long colonnaded street. A man led a mule laden with wicker baskets uphill. Old women sat against the walls with piles of fruit and flowers. Orange blossoms scented the air and mingled with the dust and the rattles and fumes of ancient cars.

'I'm afraid my husband wouldn't think of closing the store on a Saturday for nothing more important than my arrival,' Mrs. Edwards said. 'We'll have to take a taxi.'

The taxi Mrs. Edwards hailed for them was decrepit. Its upholstery had been torn in many places and the padding leaked out in grimy little tufts.

'You'll find things a bit run-down in Manalos,' Mrs. Edwards said. 'Everything.'

Elizabeth watched the city pass by the taxi's windows. It was a very Victorian-looking town, despite the banana trees and the liana blossoms and the dirt everywhere. She saw mule carts and a few men on horses. Many of the men wore the white trousers and shirts that were apparently the tropical costume, but whereas Captain Drayton's had been immaculate, most of these were not.

They passed a little white church, castellated, and what looked like a Renaissance palace. 'That's the opera house,' Mrs. Edwards said. 'In the boom days the rubber barons used to import entire opera companies. Caruso, Schumann-Heink, Alma Gluck, I don't know who all. Sometimes the singers would perform complete operas for an audience of six or seven, I'm told. Of course, there hasn't been an opera there for thirty or forty years.'

They had come to a residential section of big stone houses with gardens and pillared porticoes. Some of the houses, trimmed with much gingerbread, reminded Elizabeth of San Francisco. Clearly many of these were mansions, although it appeared some of them had been divided into flats.

'Here we are,' Mrs. Edwards said. They pulled up in front of a little crumbling house with Corinthian pillars and a broken window on the second story — but there were flowers everywhere, offsetting the aura of decay. They had almost to push their way through a bush of jasmine that threatened to block the walk to the front door.

Mrs. Edwards's son, Denny, came out to greet them. He was a bright, freckled boy of about ten, with dark wavy hair, and he was obviously happy to see his mother. He eyed Elizabeth with friendly curiosity.

'Miss Parker will be staying with us,' Mrs. Edwards explained, leading the way into the house. 'Go fetch her bags and put them in the front room upstairs. And where are your manners? Tell Miss Parker she's welcome.'

Elizabeth laughed, because she liked

the other woman's down-to-earth friend-liness. 'Please, call me Elizabeth,' she insisted.

'Fair enough, if you'll call me Ruth. Elizabeth Parker. That's a pretty name. English, I would have said.'

'Pure American mixed stock.'

'So am I. Orrin's English. You'll find most of the population here is mixed — European and American. You'll get all confused as to who wants to be called Senhor, which is the Portuguese address, or the Spanish Señor, and who is Mister, or even Monsieur. The barons, the families that made their money on the old plantations, were mostly Americans and English, and most of them went by Mister.'

'What about the Draytons?'

They had come into a big old-fashioned-looking kitchen that Elizabeth would not have been surprised to find in any city in the States. As they talked, Ruth busied herself making a pot of coffee.

'They're a mixed bag. Kitty and her sister Maria are Deodoras, and you'd

40

think that would mean old Portuguese aristocracy, wouldn't you, but their family was English until her grandmother married a local man. He was no blue blood, either, I'll tell you that. Anyway, they let on afterwards that they were native royalty of something. Of course, Kitty herself married European stock. Her first husband was a Mr. Prescott, Walter Prescott, an Englishman, and after his death she married Karl Drayton. Karl grew up in one of the settlements up the river, but he's more or less European stock.'

'I suppose by this time her daughter would be looked upon as pure Brazilian.'

Ruth gave her a quick glance. 'Kitty has no daughter.'

'But she led me to believe . . . '

'I know, she probably talked about Caroline. Her little girl, I suppose she called her. But Caroline isn't her daughter, she's the daughter of one of the maids at the palace. The Bishop's Palace — that's what they call their house.'

'The Bishop's Palace?'

'Oh, the Bishop did live there, when

the town was booming and the church was getting her share of the pie. But when things fell through, the church had to make economies too. The Deodoras lost a house to fire and they had been supporting the church pretty generously, so they up and bought the Bishop's Palace and it's been their home ever since. Anyway, Kitty has always wanted a child, I suspect, but she never had one. So she's sort of adopted Caroline, and she talks of her as if Caroline were her own.'

'That's very fortunate for the little girl.'

Ruth sniffed disdainfully; she had no great opinion of Kitty Drayton. 'If you call it fortunate that a bright little girl who might have been nice enough if left alone has been spoiled rotten instead. But there, the child's going to be one of your students after all. I shouldn't prejudice you against her. Come on, I'll show you your room.'

A long hallway led straight down the length of the building and up a dimly lighted stairway.

'Perhaps,' Elizabeth said, 'now that she's remarried, Mrs. Drayton will have a child of her own.'

Ruth Edwards laughed out loud. 'Oh my,' she said. 'Well, I suppose it is possible, of course, if he were to decide he wanted one and if she were to convince herself that Drayton was as good a name as Deodora, which in her mind it assuredly is not.'

She was still chuckling when they reached the upstairs hall. 'On top of which, you'd have to think Kitty would be up to the nuisance of having a child, which I doubt. Far easier, from her point of view, just to take over someone else's.'

'I gather Mr. Drayton is not from the old aristocracy,' Elizabeth said.

'In the first place,' Ruth said, 'Drayton was only his father's name.

'Wasn't it his mother's? . . . Oh.'

Ruth nodded her head. 'Exactly. Karl was a river boy. There's scores of them — illegitimate children, poor little beggars, making a life for themselves as best they can along the riverfront. Only, Karl was just a little smarter than most and he had a little more backbone. He educated himself pretty well as a young one and then got himself a job on a riverboat. Worked himself up in the company, although it wasn't much of a company then; it was falling apart like everything else around here. But he got to be captain of a boat and that way he met Kitty Deodora, and first thing you know, they're married.'

'She's still pretty. I imagine she was even prettier then. Probably he fell in love at first sight.'

Ruth gave her a shrewd look. 'That's one way of looking at it. And of course he's not so very hard on the eyes himself, if you hadn't noticed.' She shrugged. 'You can't blame him, anyway, for wanting to make something of himself. And it wasn't entirely selfish. He had a lot of ideas for how to improve the company, and with Kitty's money he bought it and has rebuilt it into a highly profitable business, so in the long run Kitty benefited too. What's more, he tried to put some of the lands owned by the Deodoras that used to be rubber plantations into growing rice and peppers, which he thinks he can make profitable for the growers around here. But Kitty squelched that idea, for whatever reason. Here we are.'

They came into a large and airy room, with a huge bed surrounded by mosquito netting and a red-and-green carpet that was worn in spots. Ruth went directly to the window.

'You can see the river from here.' She looked and said, more to herself, 'I see the *Fair Lady* has gone on already. Kitty's jealous of that boat. She's jealous, period. I would think if some woman made a play for Karl, Kitty wouldn't stop at killing.'

She said that so casually that Elizabeth couldn't say for certain whether it was meant as a hint or not. She remembered the look Kitty had given her when she came on deck and saw Elizabeth having an innocent conversation with Captain Drayton. Yes, probably Kitty would murder if she thought she must to keep her man.

And that does not concern me in the least, she told herself firmly. And it was plainly none of her business what sort of problems Mr. Drayton and his wife had. She wasn't sure how long the Draytons had been married, but he was still young enough that he might have been more foolish than conniving when he decided to marry Kitty. He might even have been genuinely in love with her once, although she did not believe he was now.

She set herself to unpacking the bags Denny had brought up for her. Ruth sat on one corner of the bed and watched with unabashed curiosity.

'What a lovely figure you have,' Ruth said, holding up one of Elizabeth's dresses to admire it, although it was a plain one that Elizabeth had made herself several years ago. 'I couldn't even get this fastened around my waist. Of course, bearing three children and living in this climate will spoil anyone's figure, take warning. You go to fat far too easily in the tropics.'

'Denny's not the only child, then? Will I have the others in school too?'

Her hostess suddenly went silent. She handed the dress to Elizabeth.

'No,' she said, her voice gone soft, 'I lost two of them. Little Orrin died of malaria when he was just six, and David was bitten by a snake and died. The jungle took them, that's what I usually say. They died the same year, and that was when I turned into an old woman.'

'I wouldn't call you old.'

'I'm thirty-six. It sounds young, but to me it's not. I don't care much. I don't care about anything, really, except I pray God lets me keep Denny, at least until he grows up.' She got up from the bed and made a gesture as if dusting herself off. 'I have to get my own things unpacked, and I ought to be thinking of dinner for Orrin — he likes to have it waiting when he gets home. Later, we'll take you over and show you the school, if you like.'

When she had gone, Elizabeth found herself thinking what a nice person Ruth was. Which brought her thoughts back to the only other person she knew here, Kitty Drayton. Probably she was being unfair in deciding so quickly that she disliked Kitty.

Perhaps they could even be friends, just as Kitty insisted.

3

She had arrived on Saturday and since the school had no teacher until she began, Elizabeth saw no reason why she should not begin Monday. She told Kitty this when she came by on Sunday, and Kitty took her to see Senhor Orniz, president of the school board and officially her employer. They met at the school itself, a large building with many classrooms.

'You'll be in here,' Senhor Orniz said, bringing her into one of the larger rooms. It was filled with neat rows of student desks, with a large oak desk at the front, and behind it a blackboard. Someone had written in different colors of chalk and with a very fine hand, 'Mighty oaks from little acorns grow,' and added a garish, colourful border all around.

'That was the work of our previous schoolteacher, Miss Partridge,' Senhor Orniz said, beaming with pride. 'She was

48

very artistic. It was a pity she could not stay with us. All the local people used to come on exhibition night to see her blackboards.'

'What happened to Miss Partridge?' Elizabeth asked.

'She was captured by headhunters.'

Elizabeth turned pale, but Kitty laughed and said, 'Senhor Orniz, you're being naughty; you mustn't put it that way. He doesn't mean, Liz dear, that they came into town and carried her away. Miss Partridge allowed herself to be persuaded to go on an archaeological expedition during vacation, and the group was apparently taken by hostile natives. But this happened hundreds of miles from here, so you mustn't worry yourself over it.'

'I see,' Elizabeth said, and hastily changed the subject. 'And what are exhibition nights?'

'Just what they sound like,' Kitty said. 'The local folks all come in and you exhibit your pupils' accomplishments. Of course every parent thinks his child should do best, which requires a certain amount of diplomacy on the part of the teacher, but I know you can handle that sort of thing.'

* * *

Elizabeth came into the classroom on Monday morning to find herself facing a roomful of students of varying ages, all of whom clearly knew more than she did about the usual routine. They had been without a teacher for some time and although Senhor Orniz and a few volunteers had kept things more or less moving along, the students had gotten used to being undisciplined.

'If,' Elizabeth addressed them, 'a clerk in a store had three apples . . . '

One of the children interrupted her. 'The local stores don't carry apples.'

'Nevertheless,' Elizabeth said, 'the arithmetic will come out the same. I want someone to work this problem for me. You — let me see . . . Margarite, isn't it?'

'Margarita,' the little girl said in a cool voice.

'Very well, Margarita. Now, if a clerk in a store had three apples . . . '

'Miss Partridge always read to us before arithmetic,' Margarita informed her.

'Miss Partridge is no longer with us, and my preference is to begin with arithmetic.'

A plump, tawny-skinned girl who looked to be about six years old stood up dramatically, as if to make an announcement. Surprised, Elizabeth said, 'Yes, what is it?'

'My name is Caroline Potter,' the child declared loudly. 'I live at the Bishop's Palace with Miss Kitty, and I am to let you know right away who I am.'

'Well, I'm very happy to meet you, I'm sure. And now, if you don't mind, will you sit down please, so that we can get on with the arithmetic?'

'I don't want to sit in this seat. I want to sit in that chair by the window.'

'But Nancy is already sitting in the chair by the window.'

'It isn't Nancy, it's Denise, and she can sit here, in this chair.

'I always sit in this chair,' Denise cried, jumping to her feet as well.

'Miss Partridge always let me sit wherever I wanted,' Caroline said with a menacing glare at Elizabeth.

'Perhaps she did,' Elizabeth said, her patience wearing thin, 'but I am not Miss Partridge and I want you to stay just where you are, and to sit down at once.'

'Miss Kitty said you would be nicer than Miss Partridge, but you aren't, and I don't like you,' Caroline said, but she sat as ordered.

Elizabeth found most of the pupils helpful and willing, and Ruth's boy, Denny, did whatever he could to help her along, so that after a rocky start the day did not go too terribly.

Kitty came later in the day to watch the last of the classes and to take Caroline home. 'How did it go?' she asked, waiting by Elizabeth's desk while Caroline gathered her things together.

'I don't like Miss Parker,' Caroline said loudly. 'She wouldn't let me sit by the window, and it got so hot in here I couldn't breathe.'

Elizabeth had seen no evidence of Caroline's having any trouble with her breathing, but Kitty immediately asked, alarmed, 'Is that true?'

'It's true I wouldn't let her sit by the window, as someone else was already sitting there, but . . . '

'Oh, dear, and Caroline isn't healthy, you know. If she was having trouble with her breathing, she ought to have been allowed to sit by the window. I can't see that it would matter so much to the other child.'

Elizabeth came close to saying she thought it mattered as much to the other child as it did to Caroline, whose breathing seemed quite normal, but at Kitty's urging, she agreed reluctantly that the following day she would allow Caroline to sit by the window.

'I think that will be better all around,' Kitty said, mollified. 'Oh, and I want you to come to the house now for tea. I'm having some friends in and it will be a good time for you to meet them.'

'I'd love to come,' Elizabeth said. 'I'll just clean up first and be along shortly.'

'I'll send a taxi for you.'

* ★ ★

Within the hour Elizabeth was climbing down from a dilapidated taxi in front of the Bishop's Palace. It was close enough after all that she could as easily have walked if she had known the way.

Worn pineapples had been carved into the gateposts of the wall that surrounded the house. At first Elizabeth wasn't sure how she was to approach, but one of the rusted iron gates stood open and she went in that way, through a grove of sweet-smelling trees, and beyond them stood the house itself, looking at first glimpse like a great block of stone, and more like something built for a nobleman than for a dignitary of the church.

The palace exuded a regal air, but like nearly everything else in the city it was crumbling; its walls, four stories tall, blotched with lichen. She remembered an old cemetery back home with enormous family tombs, and this somehow reminded her of that.

She went up a flight of stone steps and banged the immense bronze knocker at the door. In a moment a mulatto girl opened the door to peer out timidly. When Elizabeth told her who she was, the girl smiled nervously and swung the door wide.

Elizabeth found herself in a big hall paved with badly cracked marble, and unfurnished except for a huge mirror in a gilt frame. The single window had been shuttered against the afternoon sun so that everything was in shadows.

The maid said something in Portuguese and left. For a moment Elizabeth was alone in the hall, with only her own pale reflection in the mirror. As she glanced at that, something moved in the depths of the glass. She looked over her shoulder to find Captain Drayton behind her.

'You look . . . ' He hesitated. 'Frightened, almost. Am I so frightening to look upon?'

'No.' She felt awkward, and she was once again aware of him as a man. 'I . . . I thought you weren't back until tomorrow.'

'I only just arrived. I got impatient.'

Silence fell between them. She tried to think of something neutral to say. 'I hope there was no family crisis that necessitated your quick return,' she managed.

'No. It was more ... more of a personal nature.'

Elizabeth heard the click of high heels along a passageway overhead. She looked toward a flight of pink marble stairs and saw Kitty Drayton appear at the top.

'Liz,' Kitty said, starting down. 'And Karl. How nice of you to entertain our guest until I could come. Liz, dear, I hope he hasn't said anything to offend you. He's like a bear when he first gets back from a trip.'

Elizabeth looked up into Karl's face and again she had that odd sense of familiarity between them. She thought she saw the faintest ghost of a smile hovering about his lips. As Kitty joined them the smile, if it had been there at all, was gone altogether.

He said good day to Elizabeth and gave a little half-bow to his wife, and was gone.

*   *   *

Elizabeth was quite surprised when she came into the room with Kitty to discover that there was no one there yet but the two of them. The tea with little sandwiches was laid on a lace cloth atop a highly polished table.

'You seemed to be enjoying quite a tête-à-tête with Karl,' Kitty said.

'As a matter of fact, he had just strolled into the hall and found me there. I think we rather startled one another.'

'I doubt that,' Kitty said. 'My husband is always calm and collected.'

Elizabeth seated herself on a hard gilt settee. Kitty sat facing her and poured their tea.

They were in an enormous high-ceilinged room with dark old wood panelling, mildewed in patches. The furnishings were elaborate period pieces, polished like satin but showing signs of wear and mildew. The expensive gold-patterned curtains looked rotted. A tremendous cut-crystal chandelier hung from the distant ceiling. Great leather-bound books and boxes, some of them clasped in brass and monogrammed, stood around the room on countless rosewood desks and tables, and on the walls were gilt-framed portraits that Elizabeth took to be the Deodora ancestors.

Elizabeth sipped her tea while Kitty chattered, identifying some of the portraits, explaining how various pieces of furniture had been transported from Europe by ship and through the jungles in caravans.

A spinsterish-looking woman in a bland gray dress came into the room. She looked uncertain whether to stay or go until Kitty included her in the party with a sweeping gesture.

'Come and meet our guest, Maria dear,' she said. 'Liz, this is my sister, Maria Deodora.'

Elizabeth stood and shook hands with the frail creature, hoping her surprise hadn't been too evident. Kitty had told her that Maria was a few years older than she was, but of course Kitty looked so young that it was a great shock to realize this withered creature was her sister and not her mother. Maria must have still been shy of fifty, but she looked ten, even fifteen years older.

'Have you had your tea, Maria?' Kitty asked.

'No, I've just come from the theater.' Maria sat down stiffly, not at the table with them but in a window seat and removed her hat, of a gray that did not quite match her dress. She stabbed it with small silver hatpins and laid it on the seat beside her.

'Did you enjoy the play?' Kitty asked. 'It was that Congreve thing, wasn't it?'

'Yes. I liked it, a bit,' Maria said.

'I find Congreve too dry,' Kitty said sharply. From below, the door knocker sounded loudly. Maria stiffened.

'That will be Clark,' Kitty said to Elizabeth. 'He's the lead actor in our local theater group. A very pleasant young man, very talented, and quite handsome too. I thought the two of you should meet one another.'

Someone to occupy the schoolmistress, so that she and Captain Drayton might not be 'startling' one another?

Footsteps echoed in the marble corridor outside and in a moment the maid opened the door to whisper, 'Mr. Bennet, Senhora.'

Maria remained sitting, the window light behind her, her face a pink blur against the faded gray of her hair and her dress. Kitty rose, however, erect and absolute, and advanced across the acreage of moldy carpet.

'Come in, Clark, come in,' she said in her most splendid voice. 'Sit down. I want you to meet Elizabeth Parker. Liz is our new school teacher and she and I are already great friends. Isn't she lovely?'

Embarrassed, Elizabeth stood too and offered her hand. Her first impression was that he was too handsome to be true, but she quickly realized he was nowhere near as confident as he tried to appear. She guessed that he was no more than twenty-five years old. His face crinkled into those ready-made signs of charm that such very good-looking people can sometimes assume without anything at all taking place in their heads or their hearts.

'I'm late,' he said to Kitty, 'but Senhora Costa wanted to discuss next week's play. Am I forgiven?' He favored Kitty with a flashing row of perfect teeth and looked altogether sure of the forgiveness.

Kitty turned to Elizabeth. 'Mr. Bennet is our theater's leading man. We have rather a nice group, you know. We must go one day next week, the two of us. They're doing one of those modern things then. I'll expect you'll like that more than Mr. Congreve, won't you?'

Conversation went smoothly after that. Elizabeth thought she had Clark Bennet pegged rather clearly in her mind: fashionable ladies' darling, tea-party and cocktail-party pet. Clearly she was expected to express delight and wonderment at his calling and his exotic presence, and she did so with some moderation. He did not seem to mind the moderation. He warmed to her and began to talk of himself, apparently confident of her interest in the subject.

She suspected too that he was grateful for someone of his own age group with whom he could talk. Kitty, after all, for all her childish actions, was old enough to be his mother, and Maria could hardly be considered a youthful companion.

Like most actors, Clark Bennet was easy to talk to, and his favorite subject was himself. Kitty took part in the conversation as well, but Maria hardly spoke at all. In her gray outfit, sitting somewhat apart at the window seat, she seemed almost another of the shadows that had begun to lengthen in the room as day moved toward evening.

Kitty finally seemed to remember her sister. She said in the same voice she had used earlier with the maid, 'Maria, Potter promised to bring Caroline up to visit with our guests. Go and see what's keeping her.'

Maria rose without comment and went on the errand, disappearing from the room.

'Poor, poor Caroline,' Kitty said. 'If she did not live here where I could look after her, I can't think what would become of her. Her mother is such a scatterbrain.'

Elizabeth had her own ideas of what might become of little Caroline if she were removed from Kitty's care, but she kept them to herself.

Maria returned a few minutes later with Caroline in attendance. The child looked sullenly at Elizabeth.

Maria had brought a plate of cookies. Kitty snatched the plate from her. 'Let Caroline serve them. She does it so sweetly.'

Caroline said in a whining voice, 'I

don't want to give them to Miss Parker. I don't like her.'

'Caroline, darling!' Kitty looked shocked.

Elizabeth rose quickly. 'It's all right,' she said evenly. 'I don't mind and, really, I must be going. Ruth — Mrs. Edwards — expects me back for dinner and I'm sure it will be ready soon.'

Mr. Bennet rose too and took Elizabeth's hand, to say warmly, 'I hope you'll come to see one of my plays.'

'We'll all come next week,' Kitty declared loudly. She beamed upon the two of them.

Elizabeth, who thought things would go rather more smoothly if Kitty believed she had an interest in the actor, said, 'Yes, I would like that,' and made her departure.

Outside, she turned and looked back at the Bishop's Palace. As she did so, she saw a curtain at one of the upstairs windows flutter. Had someone in that vast house been watching her?

Kitty? Or Maria, that pale ghost of her forceful sister?

Or might it have been Karl Drayton?

4

Elizabeth knew that her success in Manalos would depend upon pleasing Kitty Drayton, and she tried to do so. Her father had often warned her, however, that she was too independent-acting and too quick-tempered. It was inevitable that she and Kitty clash sooner or later.

For the most part, the days went along without incident. The faces she saw each day became less strange to her and began to have names attached to them. She was more or less comfortable at the Edwards' house. Ruth was friendly but Elizabeth knew that Orrin was not altogether happy having her there, with the result that she did not stay around much when he was at home.

She got along well enough at school. Not a total success, but the children had decided to do as she said, except for Caroline, who could generally be counted on to insist on doing just the opposite.

She did go with Kitty and Maria the following week to see a play, *The Glass Menagerie*, by Mr. Tennessee Williams. The theater was old and decaying, as was to be expected, haunted by the ghosts of its former days. They sat at the front of the dress circle. Kitty and Maria, despite the warmth of the day, wore gowns and furs. Elizabeth, having neither furs nor a gown, had worn one of her schoolroom outfits.

Ruth had already explained to Elizabeth that Kitty Drayton was the theater's biggest sponsor. Kitty said before the play began, 'Walter — my first husband — was a great lover of the theater, and he sponsored this one lavishly. He was a very brilliant man, of impeccable tastes. You would have enjoyed him. Of course, he never had a moment for any other woman. He was devoted to me.'

'Does Captain Drayton come to the theater often?' Elizabeth asked.

Kitty laughed lightly. 'Karl's not the theater type. He's so busy with his boats all the time. But at least I don't have to worry about his having another woman either — his boats are his mistresses. Not that I mean to imply he would do that sort of thing anyway,' she said a bit more sternly. 'He's devoted to me too, in his way. Not as emphatically as Walter was, but then Walter was a unique man. Don't you think, Maria?'

Maria's answer was a barely audible, 'Surely.'

Karl Drayton seemed to be compared often to Kitty's first husband and found wanting. Elizabeth couldn't help wondering why Kitty had fallen in love with the river man if he was such a poor second to the deceased Mr. Prescott.

The play made up in theatrics what it lacked in sense. Clark Bennet was rather what Elizabeth had expected — a little more than competent, and a shade less than brilliant. He flashed and postured and displayed all the trickery and easy confidence of a well-trained actor with no great natural talent. She enjoyed his performance nonetheless, and the small audience was enthusiastic.

Kitty had tears streaming down her face when the play was over. 'He's another Barrymore,' she exclaimed, dabbing at her eyes with a lace handkerchief.

Maria had relaxed and gone a little limp. Her face was expressionless, shut down, as a morning glory flower shuts itself down when the sun goes.

Afterward, they went round to Clark's dressing room and even Elizabeth, who after all had not been quite so awed as the rest of the audience seemed to have been, felt important being able to visit the leading man in his dressing room.

He was pleased to see them, sweeping a dressing gown off a battered chair for Kitty to sit on and offering a dressing-table stool to Maria. He invited Elizabeth to sit atop an old trunk, the only seating left, but she insisted she really wanted to stand after sitting so long.

Clark offered Elizabeth a cigarette, which she declined, and she was happy that he decided not to smoke either. He waited for his visitors to tell him how good he had been. He looked almost too brilliant, with his stained crimson dressing gown over his shirt and trousers. He ran a plastic comb through his dark curls.

Beads of sweat shone on his eyebrows and upper lip and his shirt stuck damply to his body. Elizabeth was reminded of her first glimpse of Karl Drayton, sweating as well, his clothes clinging almost obscenely to his body — but Captain Drayton had projected an overwhelming, almost frightening masculinity that Clark Bennet could only play-act.

'Well, what did you think of it?' Clark asked finally. 'Like it?'

It was clear to Elizabeth that it was not the show on which he wanted their opinion. Elizabeth felt that he had earned his supper. 'Your performance left us all utterly speechless,' she said.

'Really?' He asked questions and she gave him the answers he wanted to hear, with no need for deception. It had been a workmanlike performance.

'I can see why you're popular,' she summed it all up.

'Clark is indeed very popular here,' Kitty said, beaming. 'Isn't he, Maria?'

'Yes, very,' Maria agreed. In the mirror Elizabeth saw Maria pick up the comb that Clark had put down a minute before.

She ran her fingers absently over the teeth.

Elizabeth glanced at Kitty and saw that she had seen the gesture too. There was something very ugly, like gloating, in the smile that flitted briefly over her face before she turned away.

★ ★ ★

Elizabeth had gotten in the habit of going for walks by herself when school was out. Usually she took the street that led to a point on the river slightly above the landing. Aside from the boats of the Drayton line, there were other vessels that sometimes came to the landing bearing produce from the plantations, or sometimes the launch of a party of explorers. One day a photographic party from an American magazine came and spent several hours taking pictures.

Strangely, she found it was not the people from her past — few as they had been — that she missed, or the activities. She missed the night-time sky of the city, when it was bruised blue and gray and purple by the multicolored lights — stores, bars, traffic signals. Night when it fell here was too dark, and she rarely went out after sundown.

Manalos was not on the Amazon, but on the smaller Rio Negro, and almost at the juncture of the two. The dark waters from which the river took its name changed with different lights and different times of day. In the early morning the water might shine gold with the reflection of the morning sun. Later it was a dark green-brown, growing darker as twilight approached and the shadows grew long. Occasionally at sunset the water was all pink and mauve, with an opalescent quality like something out of a fairytale. She did not much care for Manalos yet, but she thought the river beautiful in its eerie way.

On Sunday morning she left early for a stroll. She did not choose to attend church services, although Kitty Drayton had hinted broadly that it would make a good impression. The truth was, the week just past had been a trying one and she felt the need for solitude.

When she came in sight of the landing, however, she saw that the *Fair Lady* was in. Captain Drayton had been away on a run, as he generally seemed to be. It gave her an inexplicable sense of pleasure to see the boat and know that he was in town, though it was unlikely that she would see the man himself.

But she did see him only a moment later, when he and Captain Warren came along the street from the river toward her. They saw her and Captain Warren waved. She waited for them to come up to where she was.

'How's the prettiest girl along the Amazon?' Captain Warren asked. 'Do you mean to tell me none of the young men around here have proposed to you yet?'

She laughed and said, 'The oldest one in my class is fourteen, which I find a little young for my tastes.'

'Good morning,' Captain Drayton greeted her a bit more formally.

'Good morning. If you're on your way home, I'm afraid you'll find everyone is at church.'

Captain Warren said, 'That's good, I'll

have an hour of peace with no one there to nag at me.'

Elizabeth laughed again. In the short time she had been here, she knew already that the city boasted no more devoted couple than the Warrens.

'Give my respects to Mrs. Drayton,' Captain Warren said to Karl. He tipped his hat to Elizabeth and went off down the street. Elizabeth found herself unexpectedly alone with Captain Drayton.

There were people around to be sure, even at an early hour on Sunday morning, but the bustle of the street and the nearby landing were only a backdrop for the moment when she turned and found his eyes studying her intently.

'Where were you going just now?' he asked.

'Only for a walk along the river.'

'I'll come with you,' he said and when she hesitated, he asked, 'What's the matter?'

'Nothing,' she said, beginning to walk.

Suddenly nothing was the matter. It was a magnificent morning. For just a second or two she'd had a sense of impending disaster, a warning that comes sometimes when one is about to do something important, something that later you will not be able to undo.

She wondered if the man at her side had felt the same sense of warning. He had waited politely for her to decide, but she sensed that he was only seeming to defer to someone else's will when in reality he would act strictly according to his own.

'How is it you did not go to church?' he asked.

'I'm not Catholic.' At the moment the city offered a choice between Catholicism and the high-zeal Protestantism of a missionary church.

'You were brave to accept this job thousands of miles from home, in a completely strange place,' he commented.

'We are brave when there is nothing else to be. I hadn't any alternatives.'

'I think there are always alternatives, but they can be challenging.'

They had come to the edge of town. The walk along the river petered out into a path through thick grass that soon became the jungle itself. On the opposite bank the trees came right down to the water.

On their side an empty rowboat had been drawn up to the narrow, muddy bank. Two dogs played in the long grass. They ran into the water and came back to shake themselves, sending a spray of water for several feet.

'It's a beautiful morning,' she said.

'And do you find Brazil beautiful?'

'Perhaps. There's a sense of . . . bigness, I suppose. Did you always want to go on the river?'

'Yes. When I was little it meant escape, but as I got older I learned that it's not any good to run away. You have to start right where you are, building something. That's the only way.'

He had taken off his cap and where the sun had bleached it, the tips of his brown curls were nearly the same color as his deeply tanned skin. She suddenly thought he looked very young and far less formidable than she had always thought of him. But she did not think this man beside her would ever be afraid of anything.

'All of this waste,' he said out of the blue, indicating with one gesture of his hand the surrounding jungle and the decaying city of Manalos itself, 'because they cling to the past and refuse to accept reality. Manalos and Brazil could be rich today, far richer than in the past, if they would only strive for progress, only see that the past is gone.'

It suddenly occurred to her that they had been here longer than they should be. 'We must be going back,' she said, glancing at her watch. 'You'll miss Kitty and Caroline at church.'

'I won't miss them.'

She did not want to go back either. It had been a long time since she had felt happy. She had been alone since her father's death, and now she did not feel alone, and she knew that when they parted and she returned to Ruth's house and her room on the second floor, she would feel alone again.

She looked at him and found him again studying her intently. One of the dogs, a black mongrel, had discovered them and came to where they stood, begging for a little attention. She reached down absent-mindedly and petted him, and his tail wagged mightily to and fro.

'I really think we had better go,' she said.

They started back the way they had come, the dog trotting along with them. Sometimes he would run ahead or fall behind, as something or other caught his fancy, but he soon fell into step again.

'I wonder if he has a home?' she asked. 'If we only had a little more time, we could make this friendship permanent.'

'Yes.'

She had meant the friendship with the dog, but the tone of his voice told her he meant something far different.

'I'll be leaving right away again,' he said. He did not sound happy about it.

'You're lucky. It's a lovely day to be traveling. I wish I were going with you.'

To her great surprise, he said, 'Come along, then.'

'Oh, no, I must stay here and teach spelling and arithmetic.'

'You don't like it here, do you?' he asked, looking down at her as they walked.

'I don't mind the city. I just have no sense of belonging. I feel so isolated. I don't know how to put it better.'

'I understand.'

They had neared the church. The bells began to ring, signaling the end of the service. 'You'll have to hurry,' she said. 'Goodbye.'

He took her hand in his. He did not say goodbye but stood holding her hand, regarding her in silence, and after a moment she drew her hand away and turned from him, walking quickly up the street toward the Edwards' house. She did not look back, but somehow she knew he was watching her go.

* * *

Later, when she came down to lunch, she saw that there was some tension in the air between Ruth and her husband, Orrin. He looked angry and Ruth was nervous.

'Elizabeth,' Ruth said, 'what's this awful story we hear about your keeping Karl Drayton so busy promenading with you that he didn't make it to church to join his wife?'

She said it in a joking manner but she spoke much too rapidly. Elizabeth glanced at Orrin. He was regarding her solemnly.

'Someone saw the two of you,' Ruth said.

'I met Captain Warren and Captain Drayton near the landing,' Elizabeth said. She was angry and she spoke very precisely to control it. 'Captain Drayton did not want to go into the church in the middle of the service, which had already begun, and asked if he might walk with me for half an hour until church got out so that he could meet his wife. I see nothing strange in that.'

'Oh dear, no,' Ruth said, 'I know you meant nothing by it. But you know how people gossip. Old Senhora Menoz, she wasn't able to get to church this morning because of her arthritis, and she saw you and called us in on our way home. She's an awful busybody.'

'She was only telling the truth,' Orrin said in an angry voice. 'As for Captain Drayton's intentions, you may as well know, he didn't meet his wife after church. She wouldn't even have known he was here, I suppose, if Senhora Menoz hadn't seen him gallivanting with you.

And as for you, you ought to remember that a schoolteacher is a person of some responsibility. You oughtn't to go strolling out in the jungle with a married man like you were a dance-hall entertainer.'

'Orrin!' Ruth looked shocked.

'It's all right,' Elizabeth said. She went out of the room without saying more. She did not want to quarrel with them, and when she came down again later she acted as if nothing had happened.

Ruth, too, chose to ignore their little quarrel, except that the following day, apropos of nothing, she said, 'Do bear in mind, Liz, Kitty is totally ruthless. If she ever got it into her mind that you were a rival for Karl's affections, well, there's no telling what she might do.'

'But I am not,' Elizabeth said, and the subject was dropped.

Later, Elizabeth was to wish that she had taken the warning more seriously.

5

When Elizabeth came in from school the following day, she found Kitty Drayton sitting in the kitchen with Ruth. In an elaborate hat and her elegant prune-and-cream striped dress, Kitty looked out of place in Ruth's old-fashioned kitchen.

'Liz, honey,' Kitty greeted her, 'we've been talking about you, haven't we, Ruth?'

'We've been talking about lots of people,' Ruth said, stirring cake batter in a large brown bowl. She did not look at Kitty or Elizabeth.

Elizabeth saw at once that Kitty appeared a little too bright. She had come to recognize that brightness: it meant that Kitty was about to indulge in one of her reckless impulses and do something that she knew others would not approve of.

'I've just been telling Ruth,' Kitty said gaily, 'that I think it's foolish for you to stay on like you are, cooped up in one little room upstairs like a common boarder, when I've got the Bishop's Palace practically to myself, with acres of room. And you have no idea how lonesome I get with Karl away so much. When Walter was here I loved the house — he was always in it with me — but honestly, sometimes now I practically hate it, I feel so alone.'

Elizabeth was completely surprised. 'But it's a very comfortable room, and I can't see any reason just to up and move . . . '

'Yes, but if Orrin is so unhappy having you here,' Kitty said, and then stopped, looking chagrined. 'Oh, I've put my foot in my mouth, haven't I?'

An awkward silence followed. Ruth had turned crimson.

'Is Orrin unhappy about my staying here?' Elizabeth asked.

'Oh, he's a fool,' Ruth said, stirring her batter with a vengeance. 'He's a worse gossip than any woman in the town. And he says people have been talking to him, hinting about taking their business elsewhere.'

Elizabeth thought she had a pretty good idea who might have been doing the hinting. Kitty Drayton's business could make or break any local merchant.

'That wasn't the point at all, though,' Kitty said. 'This is not about Orrin, it's about you and me, Liz dear. You would be doing me a favor if you would come up to the palace and stay with me, really you would. I do get lonesome, honestly.'

'You have your sister and little Caroline,' Elizabeth said. 'And a houseful of servants.'

'Oh, them.' Kitty dismissed them all with a wave of one gloved hand.

'Listen,' Ruth said, putting her bowl down with a bang. 'I'm not just going to put you out. I told Orrin that.'

'You wouldn't be putting me out,' Elizabeth said quietly. 'I'm just going up to the Bishop's Palace for a visit. It will be a wonderful experience for me, to see how the aristocracy lives.'

'Oh, well, we're pretty much like ordinary people,' Kitty said modestly. She had a triumphant look on her face. 'It's settled, then. You'll come up tomorrow.

I'll send the servants down to move your things while you're at school. You see, Ruth, I knew it would work out. I hope you'll go right over and tell that Senhora Menoz.'

'What does Senhora Menoz have to do with this?' Elizabeth asked.

'It's nothing, really,' Kitty said. 'It's just, she's such an old busybody. Can you believe it, she actually warned me about you. She said she never did trust Karl. I practically laughed in her face.'

She was talking a mile a minute. Elizabeth understood now about the invitation. It had nothing to do with Kitty's 'loneliness.' It was meant to stop any further gossip and show everyone that she and Kitty were close friends.

'I told her that you and I were the best of friends,' Kitty said. 'I said you didn't even like Karl, isn't that right?'

'I don't think I know Captain Drayton well enough to say that I like or dislike him,' Elizabeth said.

'My, you are so polite. But you needn't be, not on my account. Lots of people don't like him. They think he's uppity for marrying above his station, but they don't understand him like I do, is all. It doesn't hurt my feelings any, honest. You'll come tomorrow, then? I'll send someone for your things.'

'I'll come at the end of the week,' Elizabeth said.

'No, tomorrow, please. I want to see Senhora Menoz's face when she hears. As a matter of fact, I'll go myself and tell her right now.'

She kissed Elizabeth goodbye and left. When she had gone, Ruth said, 'Elizabeth, dear, you don't have to move, you know that. Orrin was just fussing.'

'I know, but she's probably right — this is the best way to squelch any gossip.'

She went upstairs and stood for a time at the window. She wondered where the *Fair Lady* was now. Probably halfway to Belem. It was quite a convenient thing, to leave troubles behind by walking on board a riverboat and going a thousand miles away. She could not go away — she had to stay right where she was.

Moving into the Bishop's Palace did not mean just living with Kitty. It meant that, when he returned from Belem, she would be sharing the house with Karl. The two of them, only rooms apart.

She wondered if Kitty had considered that as well.

★ ★ ★

The following day she moved into the palace. The room that Kitty had prepared for her was much finer than any she had occupied before in her life. The enormous four-poster bed, the handsome chest of drawers, and the elaborately carved armoire all looked as if they belonged in a museum.

While Kitty was showing her the room, a sullen-looking woman came in with Caroline. 'Oh, there you are,' Kitty said. 'Liz, dear, this is Potter. She's worked in the house for years, and everyone just calls her Potter. Potter, this is my dear friend, Elizabeth Parker. She's going to be staying here with us, and I want you to do everything possible to make her comfortable.'

Caroline was her usual rude self,

ignoring Elizabeth completely and opening and closing dresser drawers to poke at Elizabeth's belongings. Watching her, Elizabeth remembered that Potter was Caroline's real mother. She saw too that Potter was not happy about having her here — probably, she surmised, because she was afraid that the new intimacy between Kitty and Elizabeth might jeopardize her own obviously favored position.

Potter had brought a pitcher of water and some fresh glasses on a tray, and she set them on the dresser. 'I think that's everything,' she told Kitty in an icy voice.

Caroline, abandoning her search of the dresser, swung around to face the adults in the room. 'This is Leila's room,' she declared.

'Who is Leila?' Elizabeth asked.

'Leila is one of her dolls,' Potter said.

'She is my own little girl, and this is her bedroom,' Caroline said sharply. 'You can't send her away.'

'I'll tell you what,' Kitty said, 'we'll let her sleep in the little doll bed Uncle Karl brought from Rio.'

'No,' Caroline said again. She fixed her angry eyes on Elizabeth. 'When is she going away?'

'Caroline, honey, that's not polite,' Kitty said.

'It isn't polite of her to come and take Leila's bed. You said Leila could sleep here whenever Uncle Karl was away. Where is Uncle Karl going to sleep if he comes home and finds her sleeping in his bed?'

Kitty went scarlet. 'Caroline, what a naughty thing to say. You know Uncle Karl only sleeps in here when I'm not feeling well. Now you take Leila back to your room and not another word. Potter, I think you could keep her from being underfoot all the time. It's inconvenient for me.'

Potter mumbled, 'Sorry,' and whisked Caroline away.

Kitty looked terribly vexed. She went around the room, pushing things about and rearranging. 'I hope you didn't mind,' she said. 'She's just a child, and they do get notions in their heads.'

'She didn't hurt my feelings in the

least.' Elizabeth knew full well that was not what was agitating Kitty so.

'Potter shouldn't have brought her in here. She's such an imaginative child; I don't know where she gets those absurd ideas of hers. Let's go downstairs. You can finish settling in later.'

They sat in the parlor and had sherry, and Kitty's good humor was restored in a short while and she gossiped happily until dinnertime. Nothing more was required of Elizabeth than an occasional smile or brief comment, and for the most part her thoughts were free to roam.

She found herself thinking that the entire house had something of the quality of a dollhouse about it, but on a larger scale. None of it seemed quite real.

Which perhaps was why Karl Drayton seemed so out of place in it.

6

Karl was away for the next few days and Kitty seemed to enjoy having someone to chatter to or show off things to.

Elizabeth began to see what Kitty had meant when she had talked of being lonesome in the Bishop's Palace. Karl was apparently often gone, and Elizabeth doubted that there was much close communication between husband and wife even when he was home. Snob that she was, Kitty would have been unable to have any real friendship with the servants — who, Elizabeth noted, tended to treat her as if she were a child — and Caroline, although doted upon, could hardly have provided Kitty much in the way of companionship.

As for Maria, Elizabeth did not quite know what to make of the relationship between the two siblings. She thought Kitty treated her sister with an especial rudeness that might have been mere habit or might have been calculated.

Kitty seemed almost set upon humiliating her older sister. She treated her with less respect and consideration than she did the servants. Indeed, she often 'ordered' Maria to wait upon her in some little way or another, and if Maria went out of the house she must ring the bell when she returned for one of the servants to let her in, as she had no key of her own to the house in which she had lived since childhood.

'That's what servants are for,' Kitty said when Elizabeth asked about that oddity.

If Maria was ever so bold as to express any sort of opinion of her own, Kitty was quick to disagree with it, even belittle it. More often, however, Maria remained silent and withdrawn. She might have been expected to resent her sister's treatment of her, but if she did, it did not show in her face.

Several times Elizabeth had tried to befriend Maria, but she was so consistently rebuffed that she decided her efforts in that vein were only wasted. Maria lived in a world of her own. She read romantic novels voraciously, and collected pretty ribbons and dried flowers which she pressed in her books.

Elizabeth had learned that the family money had all been entrusted to Kitty, who had in turn to care for Maria so long as she lived. A stronger-willed woman might not have let that hold her, of course, but Elizabeth could see that Maria would regard herself as tied forever to her sister. Apparently she had resigned herself to that fact and made whatever adjustments she had needed to make in her thinking.

It was plain, though, that there was no affection or even friendship wasted between the two. Nor did Kitty have any real friends in town. She was an aristocrat and one of the town's leaders, and so had to be treated with deference, but it was easy to see that she was not liked. She was too irresponsible and too used to having things her way.

It was a strange life, then, that Kitty lived in that vast palace, having every material comfort but no friends and, for all practical purposes, no husband.

Their routine was fairly simple. Kitty always waited to have tea with her when Elizabeth returned from school. Once or twice Elizabeth did not come home directly. On one occasion she stopped to visit with Ruth, and another time she simply went for a stroll — alone this time. She returned to the palace to find Kitty presiding peevishly over a now-cold teapot, waiting with ill-concealed impatience for Elizabeth to arrive before anyone else could have tea.

Sometimes Maria would join them for tea and sometimes not. On two different occasions Clark Bennet came by after his afternoon performances at the theater. When he was not there, Kitty prattled on about how Clark was obviously smitten by Elizabeth. She seemed determined to promote a romance between the two of them.

For her own part, Elizabeth could see that Clark was interested in becoming better acquainted, but she saw too that Clark was as close as Kitty came to having a friend. She even wondered if there might be something more between them, but quickly dismissed that idea. Kitty was considerably older than Clark, for one thing, and it would have been out of character for Kitty to have an affair.

In some peculiar way, Kitty dominated the actor. There was almost a mother-and-son relationship between them. And Elizabeth did learn through Ruth, who managed to keep abreast of most of the city's gossip, that Clark was mentioned in Kitty's will.

'Of course that sort of information is strictly confidential,' Ruth added, 'but a lawyer can't be expected to keep things from his wife, and women do talk, don't they?'

As for romantic impulses, however, other than toward her husband, Kitty saved them all for the memory of her first husband, Walter.

'A more splendid man you never met,' she was fond of saying.

* * *

After dinner, Kitty and Elizabeth usually spent some time in the parlor. Ostensibly they did needlework, but Kitty's chief interest was always gossip and she had an inexhaustible fund of material. Hardly a name was mentioned about which she did not have some slightly scandalous story to share.

Throughout the evening, the house mostly remained quiet. Caroline did not join them in the evenings and quite often Maria stayed in her own rooms. The servants, once dinner had been served, disappeared. There might have been only the two of them, Elizabeth and Kitty, in all that great, rambling mansion.

'I gave the help a television,' Kitty explained when Elizabeth commented on their absence. 'They keep it in their sitting room in the basement.'

'I shouldn't imagine there'd be much to watch,' Elizabeth said.

'There isn't. It's a far cry from what one would get in the States, certainly. There are no broadcasts until evening and then only one channel. The news begins at eight o'clock, and various shows after that. It doesn't matter what's showing, though. From eight o'clock on they are almost certain to be glued to their sitting room.'

By nine Kitty was ready to retire, but there was a certain fussiness even in this. Potter, or the housekeeper Amelie, had to interrupt their television viewing to bring tea to her bedroom on a tray while Kitty soaked in a hot bubble bath. Sometimes when she emerged from the bath, but never sooner than thirty minutes, she would invite Elizabeth to have a cup of tea in her room, but more often she had her night-time tea in private and went to bed.

When Karl was at home, Elizabeth excused herself after dinner and went to her own room. Kitty usually objected and Elizabeth noted that it was not only out of mere politeness. Husband and wife rarely had any conversation together, and when they did, it more often than not took the form of a quarrel. Elizabeth did not care to sit in on those bouts and she steadfastly insisted upon leaving them alone as much as possible when Karl was in town.

For the most part it was a dull but not

unpleasant existence. Kitty was certainly eager to maintain the pretense of a profound friendship and Elizabeth thought it probably wise to go along with the pretense. Only on one occasion did she find it necessary to assert her independence. Soon after moving into the palace, she asked Kitty for a key to the house.

'But that's not necessary,' Kitty insisted. 'There's always someone to let you in. All you have to do is ring.'

'That may be so, but I won't feel at home without a key of my own.' Elizabeth had refused to be dissuaded and finally, with a put-upon air, Kitty had given in. Clark was there the following day for tea and when he was preparing to leave, Kitty produced the big old key for the front door.

'Elizabeth thinks she's going to be locked out in the streets,' she said, handing the key to Clark. 'Be a darling, Clark, and have a duplicate made of this.'

Clark gave Elizabeth a grin that said he knew just how she felt, and pocketed the key. When he came again the following day he had the original and a duplicate key with him. He gave them both to Kitty, who made a ceremony of handing the copy to Elizabeth.

'Now,' she said, too sweetly, 'are you happy?'

'I certainly feel more comfortable,' Elizabeth said. She pocketed the key and refused to be goaded into a spat.

There was one other incident in which they came close to a quarrel. Most of the servants in the house were close to Kitty's age or considerably older, and most of them had been with her since she was a child. Although she sometimes treated them cruelly, they nonetheless doted upon her. Elizabeth suspected that, despite Kitty's tantrums, she was not a good overseer, and most of the time the servants had things their own way.

Amelie, the housekeeper, had a niece, Valerie, who sometimes helped days. She was a pretty young woman, no more than seventeen, and she had a pleasant disposition. She was shy, though, and obviously in terror of Kitty who, for whatever reason, seemed harder on her than on the other servants.

On one occasion, Valerie came to collect the tea things, a task usually performed by Amelie herself. Kitty was having what she described as one of her 'nervous days,' and she had been more irritable than usual. The sight of Valerie clearing the tea table did nothing to brighten her mood.

Valerie had loaded her tray and was just turning to leave when Kitty, spying a cup and saucer she had missed, seized them up with a quick, angry movement.

'Here,' she said, and slammed them down on the tray with such violence that Valerie, already ill at ease, dropped the tray, scattering china and tea on the floor.

Kitty was beside herself, and yet it seemed to Elizabeth that she actually looked triumphant, as if she had just been searching for some excuse to show her temper.

'Now look what you've done, you clumsy fool,' she cried. She raised her hand as if she meant to slap the maid.

Elizabeth, however, was on her feet by this time and without even thinking she stepped between them.

'Stop it,' she said firmly.

Kitty was so surprised that she did indeed stay her hand and for a full moment was utterly speechless.

'It was only an accident,' Elizabeth said, embarrassed a little now at her own brashness. 'The cup was sitting behind the lamp, where she could easily miss it, and you put it down on the tray so hard it's no wonder she dropped it.'

For a moment there was an expectant tension and Elizabeth would not have been surprised if Kitty had slapped her instead, but she turned on her heel and, without a word, swept out of the room.

Valerie looked close to tears, but Elizabeth said, 'I think you had better clean that up quickly,' and went to her own room. By the time she saw Kitty again at dinner, the incident was seemingly forgotten.

Aside from these minor skirmishes, though, she and Kitty got along smoothly; and while she found the atmosphere at the palace stifling, she had to admit that every effort was made to make her comfortable. Indeed, if she had a complaint, it was that Kitty did too much, leaving Elizabeth feeling uncomfortably obligated.

At school the time was drawing near for the annual exhibition night and Elizabeth was busy preparing her pupils. Ruth had warned her that she would have to make a good impression on the parents and the school board, even if it meant providing the dull students with the answers to questions she meant to ask them. Elizabeth could not help feeling she was going to come in a poor second-best to Miss Partridge, her predecessor, whose chalk decorations had long since been washed from the blackboard.

The afternoon of the exhibition, she came in to find Karl at home and in the parlor with Kitty. Elizabeth had been so busy that she hadn't been by the landing and so had not seen the boat. She said good afternoon to him rather stiffly and would have gone on up the stairs to her room, but Kitty stopped her.

'Heavens, you needn't rush off,' she exclaimed. 'You usually sit and have tea, as I've already said to Karl, and he will think you're trying to avoid him. I've been trying to persuade him to come to the exhibition tonight. Caroline is going to perform.'

He was standing by the window. He glanced at his wife and said, 'I told you I'd go.'

'You said you supposed you might. I thought Liz would be able to persuade you more definitely.'

He looked at Elizabeth and she looked away. She had discovered that when she looked at him there was no one else in the room, and she must not do anything that would rouse Kitty's suspicions. Just now she could feel Kitty's eyes on her, like the eyes of a hungry cat watching a bird. It was a hot day. The windows were open and Kitty was fanning herself with a little Japanese fan.

Caroline was seated on a chair near Kitty, playing with a doll. Kitty said to her, 'Tell Uncle Karl what you're going to do tonight.'

'I'm going to recite 'Hiawatha', which is a poem by Mr. Longfellow. And I'm also going to win the prize in the spelling bee.' She hardly glanced up when she made this announcement.

'Of course you are, darling. Aunt Kitty donated the prize herself and she's going to be very proud when you win it.'

Elizabeth said she must go up to her room if she was to be ready for dinner. The sitting room was on the second floor but her bedroom was on the third. It was quiet up there. The shutters had been closed and sunlight lay in stripes across the carpet. She stood for a long time just inside the door of her room. She could still hear the murmur of voices from below.

She felt as if she were caught in quicksand. She could feel herself being dragged down and she knew the tragic ending that awaited her, but she could not extricate herself.

★   ★   ★

Dinner was an effort. Kitty talked at great length without really saying anything, while Elizabeth and Karl exchanged polite comments on the weather. The sun

102

was nearly down but the house was no cooler. A dark-skinned boy stood in one corner of the room pulling a cord that made a big ceiling fan go slowly back and forth above them, but it did little to make the room more comfortable.

Elizabeth found herself thinking that if it were her house, she would have suggested a cold supper on the terrace in the rear, or even in the big kitchen with its tile floors that seemed cool no matter how hot the day.

'You should have gotten a new dress to wear,' Kitty said to Elizabeth. 'We want you pretty tonight. You never know what man is going to see you. Oh, maybe you should wear the green dress I was planning to wear. It doesn't matter how an old married woman like me dresses.'

'I don't think it matters how I dress either,' Elizabeth said. 'It is parents' night and I presume that the men who are there will be married.'

She stood up to go. She had already said she wanted to be at the schoolhouse early. The truth was, she did not want to have to walk with the Draytons.

'Well, we'll all come home together,' Kitty promised. Her cheeks were flushed and she was talking too much and too rapidly. Elizabeth saw Karl glance at her as if she were not quite real.

The exhibition was not being held in the classroom they normally used for classes but in the school's auditorium. With the help of some of the students, Elizabeth had decorated it with streamers and flowers and had moved a large blackboard onto the stage for use in some of the demonstrations.

The children arrived early and she arranged them in chairs on the stage, in the order of their performances. As parents arrived she greeted them, welcoming them to the exhibition. Although by this time most of the parents had seen her about town, this was their first chance to really observe her and she knew that she was an object of some curiosity. Almost everyone came, including several who did not have children in the school.

Senhor Orniz arrived shortly before the recitations were due to begin. She saw him look in the direction of the

104

blackboard, but it was undecorated, and with a resigned sigh he went on to his chair.

The Draytons came just as Elizabeth was beginning her little welcome speech. There was some commotion as Kitty insisted on seats in the front row, although the auditorium was small and there could be no difficulty hearing or seeing even from the last row. Captain Drayton followed his wife down front, looking angry and embarrassed.

Elizabeth was all too aware that the program was long and dull. It had been necessary to include every child in something and that had taken some ingenuity. One after the other of the students stumbled through their recitations while the parents fanned themselves and tried to look interested. The room was hot and stuffy and in the intervals between recitations they could hear birdcalls from the not-too-distant jungle.

There were two spelling bees, one for the older students and one for beginners. Elizabeth knew all too well that Kitty would be upset if Caroline did not win the beginners' prize she anticipated, and although she hated herself for being a coward, she had given Caroline the easiest words she could think of.

At length the match came down to Caroline and Lorna Dalgado. They stood side by side on the stage facing the audience. Elizabeth asked Caroline to spell 'Amazon' — sure Caroline would have no difficulty spelling that.

'A-m-o-z-o-n,' Caroline said.

Elizabeth looked blankly at her for a moment. Lorna Dalgado did not wait to be asked, but quickly piped up, 'A-m-a-z-o-n.'

There was nothing Elizabeth could do but name Lorna the winner and give her the prize. But before she could do so, Caroline spoke again. 'That's what I said,' she said loudly. 'Amazon. A-m-a-z-o-n.' She looked straight into Elizabeth's eyes. The fans in the audience stopped and there was a pregnant silence.

'I'm sorry, Caroline,' Elizabeth said, 'perhaps you meant to spell it that way, but you did say 'o-z-o-n,' and I'm afraid Lorna has won the prize.' She picked up the tissue-wrapped package to hand it to Lorna, but Caroline did not return to her chair.

'I want the prize,' she said in a rising voice. 'I spelled the word right and I won the prize.'

Kitty, in the front row, stood and said, 'I must say, Liz, you're being awfully difficult. If Caroline said she spelled the word correctly, she surely isn't lying about it. You must have misunderstood her. It's easy to do with the vowels. From down here, I thought I heard Lorna say 'o' instead of 'a'.'

Someone halfway back in the audience said that Elizabeth had heard correctly. The children, who had been sitting long enough to get restless and welcome a diversion, began to debate the issue among themselves. One of them flatly told Caroline she was 'a big fat liar.'

Elizabeth could see that things were in danger of getting completely out of hand. She told the children in no uncertain voice to be quiet, and handed the prize to Lorna, telling Caroline to please take her seat.

Kitty, however, did not mean to let it lie there. 'Indeed she will not take her seat,' she said, striding up the steps to the stage. Facing her, Elizabeth realized that although Kitty sounded furious, there was an excited, almost happy glitter in her eyes. 'I will not let this child stay here and be branded a liar.' She took Caroline's hand and started for the exit.

'Kitty, please,' Elizabeth said. 'It was a simple mistake . . . '

'Indeed! And you made it,' Kitty said. She had started now and seemed determined to create a scene. 'You are mistaken if you think you are welcome to stay in my house if this is how you treat your friends.'

Karl had come up the steps to the stage as well, and as Kitty started past him toward the exit he said something that was too low for Elizabeth to hear. Kitty paid him no attention. She brushed past him and, with Caroline in tow, stormed off the stage.

7

The silence that followed Kitty's departure was deafening. Karl went out in her wake and Elizabeth was left onstage, shaken by the scene. There was nothing she could do but go on with the program which, fortunately, was nearly over.

She told Lorna to sit down and went to the side of the stage to bring out the easel on which she had placed a map of the world.

'We will have geography next,' she said. She picked up the pointer, annoyed to find that it was shaking in her hand, and began to ask the students questions about the map.

At last the program was over. There was some polite applause and then the confusion of children and parents finding one another. Ruth Edwards came up to the stage.

'You're coming home with me,' she said. 'No discussion!'

Senhor Orniz, coming up as well, said, 'It was most unfortunate.' He looked at Elizabeth with an expression as if he had just bitten into something that he realized was spoiled.

The parents were leaving rapidly. Elizabeth said good night to those who left by the stage exit. The men were embarrassed and the women cool.

Karl Drayton came back, striding purposefully along the aisle toward the stage. Several people who were on their way out stopped to see what would happen next. Senhor Orniz took a few steps toward the exit as if he meant to flee, but Karl stopped him before he could make his escape.

'Senhor Orniz, stay, please. I want you to hear this,' Karl said as he came up the steps. 'Miss Parker, I want to apologize for my wife's behavior of a few minutes ago. I'm afraid she isn't feeling well.'

Ruth said, 'I expect it's the heat. Kitty is very sensitive.' Senhor Orniz nodded quickly in agreement.

'She sent me back to apologize,' Karl said. He ignored the others and spoke

110

directly to Elizabeth. 'She did not want you to think she meant what she said, about your not being welcome at the house.'

'I've been invited to the Edwards',' Elizabeth said. 'Perhaps, Captain, it would be best if I went there.'

'I hope that you will not do so. Kitty is feeling very badly and she will feel even worse if you move out of the palace because of this.'

Senhor Orniz already looked mollified. 'The captain is right,' he said. 'We are all eager to forget this unfortunate incident.'

'You go along, honey,' Ruth said. 'Never mind about me.'

Elizabeth knew Ruth was thinking that it would look better if peace were made now, rather than letting things stand as they were, with Elizabeth turned out of the Bishop's Palace. Regrettably, Ruth was right.

'I'll get my things,' she said to Karl. She went to the cloakroom and collected her purse and a stole that she put around her shoulders, although the night was still warm. By the time she had locked up the school, the streets were very nearly empty of parents and children. For a few blocks she and Karl walked in silence.

Finally, she said, 'I hope Kitty isn't really ill.'

'No. She says she has a headache and she's gone to bed, but she wants to see you when you get there.'

'It isn't necessary. I understand. She really did want Caroline to win. I tried to help her, too, by giving her the easiest words. But sometimes these things are simply out of our hands.'

They passed a small group, two couples who had been at the program. There was a murmur of greetings as they went by.

When they were alone again he said, 'She didn't give a damn about Caroline or the spelling bee. She wanted to pick a fight with you. You know why.'

She glanced quickly up at him. 'You mean because of that gossip about our walking together? But that's nonsense. If she were worried about that, why would she send you tonight to ask me to come back to the palace?

'Sometimes it's difficult to know what

she has in that mind of hers, but I can tell you this — she never does anything without some selfish motive. I wish you hadn't agreed to come back after all.' He stopped, realizing how that sounded, then added hastily, 'For your sake, I mean.'

'I understand. But I have little choice, if I want to stop the gossip.'

They came to the wall and the open gates to the palace. He stopped and looked down at her in the moonlight. 'Let's walk some more,' he said. 'I'm leaving again tomorrow.'

'Kitty is expecting us. She'll worry.'

'She won't be worried.'

She did not want to go in. The night was warm and the moonlight was a silken presence about them. She felt as if they were isolated in this moment, in this tiny space before the crumbling wall. She could feel the gate move a little beneath her hand.

'Yes, she will be,' she said. 'If you don't want to come in, I'll say good night. I hope you have a pleasant journey tomorrow.'

'Must you always be so polite and proper?' He sounded angry. He brought his hand down hard upon the gate. 'You know nothing about it,' he said. 'She wants me to do something to upset her, to prove that she made a mistake by marrying me.'

'No. She loves you very much.'

He laughed. 'If I thought it were true I would be able to continue the charade of our marriage, but I know better. Right now she's playing the part of the devoted helpmate. Before that it was the eager bride, and before that, the fashionable widow. And she's working up to the betrayed wife. She'll be highly disappointed if she's cheated of the chance to play that part.'

Elizabeth knew she shouldn't be listening to these things, but she knew as well that they were true. Some sense of propriety, however, made her feel she should defend the absent Kitty.

'Kitty's a child. She shouldn't be judged as you would judge others.'

'She's not a child, she's a vicious jungle cat — all the more dangerous because she deludes people into thinking of her as a helpless kitten. The truth is, she's capable

of anything if she can get her way
. . . even murder. But I don't care,
frankly, as long as she doesn't hurt me, or
you. She can live her life as she chooses
and I will do the same.'

A bird stirred in a nearby tree, calling
plaintively upon the night.

Elizabeth said very firmly, 'There is
nothing I want but to live quietly. I have
had troubles enough in my life and I want
to be done with them.'

He looked steadily down at her. The
bird in the tree made a sound almost like
laughter, mocking her.

'Is that true?' he asked.

'Yes.' It was not true and she knew that
he knew it as well as she did, but it
seemed important to establish that false-
hood between them.

'A little while ago, when you said that
Kitty knows it's nothing . . . it isn't
nothing. Kitty knows that. I know it. You
know it. How can you pretend otherwise?'

'Good night,' she said. She opened the
gate and went up the walk to the door.
He had followed her and he took the key
from her and opened the door, and they

went in together.

They had hardly come in when Kitty appeared on the stairs. She wore a frilly pink negligée and her ebony hair was down about her shoulders. In the dim light she looked ghostly pale and very young.

'Oh, Liz,' she said, 'I'm so glad you came back with Karl. Wasn't that stupid of me to behave as I did? I don't know what came over me.'

'It's all right,' Elizabeth said. 'Let's forget all about it.'

'But I can't just forget it. I feel awful.' Kitty looked from Elizabeth to Karl. 'I want you to swear to me that it won't make any difference between the two of us, and that you'll stay on here at the palace. I don't know what I'd do with myself if you went away, now that we've become such good friends.'

To calm her, Elizabeth said, 'Of course I'll stay.'

Kitty clapped her hands together with a childlike pleasure. 'In a few days we'll be going down to Rio for Carnival, and you must come with me. I'll tell Senhor Orniz to close the school down so you can come.'

As Elizabeth fled upstairs to her room she heard Karl tell Kitty that something had come up and he must go down to the boat.

'You'll be back before you leave, won't you?' Kitty asked.

Elizabeth paused just long enough on the stairs to hear him say, 'No, I'll sleep on the boat and leave first thing in the morning.'

★   ★   ★

That night, Kitty came to her bedroom. Elizabeth woke with the certainty that someone was there in the room with her. She remembered the incident on the boat, when Kitty had denied coming into her room. She remembered, too, the words Karl had spoken: 'She's capable of anything if she can get her way . . . even murder.'

Some fear within her made her lie still and silent. She could smell Kitty's flowery perfume, and Kitty's breathing was loud and harsh, as if she were excited or had been exerting herself.

The mosquito netting around the bed rustled softly and then there was silence, and the perfume faded slowly. The bedroom door opened and closed with a faint click.

She was alone again.

★ ★ ★

In the morning Kitty was already making plans for their trip to Rio.

'We'll go with Karl on the boat as far as Belem,' she said, 'and fly from Belem to Rio, if you'd like. It won't be a 747 but there is a nice little service between the cities.'

'But there is the school — I think it would be better if I stayed and continued with the students.'

'Nonsense, they always get a vacation at Carnival time anyway. We'll just close up a day or two early, that's all.'

Kitty still looked excited and tense, and as if she had not slept much. Elizabeth admitted that it was cowardice on her part, but she was afraid if she refused flat out to go it would bring on another bout of temper.

'Very well then,' she relented, 'I'll go to Carnival with you.'

The days that followed were strange for Elizabeth. She and Kitty were together almost all the time except when school was in session. Kitty came to meet her when school let out and they went shopping or sometimes to the theater, or to a little tea shop that Kitty favored.

More often than not, Kitty would talk of Karl, and as she did so she watched Elizabeth closely, as though trying to discern her reactions. Several times Elizabeth did not think she could bear any further scrutiny, but she kept her silence and endured it.

Senhor Orniz, at Kitty's insistence, agreed to close the school several days earlier than usual. Elizabeth offered a mild objection, to which no one listened.

Karl had gone upriver and returned, and when he again left on the *Fair Lady* on the way down to Belem, Elizabeth and Kitty went too.

119

Clark Bennet made the trip with them. 'They're doing a play without a role for me,' he explained brightly, 'and it's ages since I had any kind of vacation.' He gave Elizabeth a grin that confirmed her suspicions that Kitty had arranged his absence.

Elizabeth wondered if Kitty thought Clark would prevent anything from happening between herself and Karl. Kitty needn't have bothered. She herself meant to see that nothing happened.

Kitty made a point their very first morning of taking her along up to the pilot house to seek out Karl. When he looked at her, when she looked at him, Elizabeth felt her pulse quicken dangerously.

'It's so lovely on the river,' she said. 'I think I'll take a turn around the boat.' She could not stay there with the two of them.

She went down to the deck below and stood at the railing. Already Manalos was out of sight and on either side of the river there was only the thick jungle to see. Captain Warren came up to where she

120

stood and greeted her cheerfully, leaning against the rail.

'I must say, these trips are certainly more pleasant with a pretty young lady along.'

She smiled. 'It must be a fine life, cruising up and down the river.'

'You sound like Karl. Every other man I know on the river is happiest when he's ashore, but not Karl. He's only himself when he's got the water under him.'

'Why is he different?' she asked. There was so much she wanted to know about Karl, and in Manalos she had not dared ask anyone because she had been afraid what they would think, but she knew that Captain Warren was a friend to both her and Karl and she need not fear what he might think of her questions.

'He's riverboat crazy. He's wanted to be on these boats since he was a little kid.'

'And now he has what he wants.'

'He has what he wants on the river, at least. Maybe that's why he doesn't like going ashore.'

'But he has a home in Manalos.'

'That's not home to him. You've been

in that house long enough to see that.'

'Yes,' she said with a sigh, grateful for his bluntness. After a pause, she asked, equally blunt, 'Why did he marry her?'

'Why would a poor young man who's never had any real experience with females marry a good-looking rich woman who goes after him with everything she's got, including a promise of his own riverboat line? Is that what you're asking me?'

'You don't like her.'

'She's a selfish, grasping snake, like one of those anacondas that live in the jungle there. They wrap themselves around their victims and crush the life from them. Karl never had a chance. I'd bet money he'd no experience with women before. And then there she was, all lace and silk and perfume, throwing herself at him.'

'But he must have loved her.'

He spat over the rail into the water. 'She never gave him time to figure things out. That boy was like a son to me and it made me sick to my stomach to watch. She had a ring on his finger before he regained consciousness from the first assault.'

'You make her sound awful. It was a fair bargain, wasn't it? He has the Drayton lines, hasn't he? As you said, at least on the river he has what he wanted.'

'Yes, he does.'

'What do you think would happen if he lost it all? Or if he gave it up?'

'He won't give it up.' He spat again. 'I'm no fool, Missy. I know that boy like I know the back of my hand. I saw how it was that first day, when the two of you laid eyes on one another. And if I could wave a magic wand and make everything the way I think it should be, you and him would cruise up and down this river together for the rest of your lives. But life isn't like that. She's never going to give him up, and if he gave her up, there'd go the boats.' He paused, and said, 'She gave him money. He gave her his youth and his innocence. Who got the better bargain?'

* * *

Later, after dark, Kitty insisted their lunch group go up to the hurricane deck where they could see the stars. Besides

Elizabeth and Kitty and Clark, there was a Mrs. Wilson and a Mr. Adams, who were both married, but not to one another.

'This is so splendid,' Kitty said, leaning against a railing with her head back so that she could stare up into the sky. The river was wide here and there were no overhanging branches of trees to block the greatness of the heavens. 'I could live on one of these boats.'

'Why don't you?' Mrs. Wilson asked. 'Seems to me it would be very romantic.'

'I can tell you why,' Mr. Adams said. 'Because what would a riverboat captain do with a wife on his arm, when everybody knows they have a girl in every port?'

'Not Karl,' Kitty said firmly. 'He's a model husband.'

'Are you so sure?' Mrs. Wilson asked in a teasing voice. 'He's so very handsome, I'm sure women throw themselves at him all the time.'

'It wouldn't do them any good.'

'I've seen enough stars,' Mrs. Wilson said. 'Let's go below and have a drink.'

It was quiet on the deck when they had gone. The boat was dark up here and the only lights were the stars and the red glare from the stacks above. Smoke and an occasional trail of sparks floated out into the air behind them. The shores had moved closer again and Elizabeth could see the dark shadows of the trees on the banks, and once the shriek of a jaguar tore the night air.

Someone came up behind her. She knew it was Karl even before she turned toward him.

'It's a nice night,' he said.

When she did turn and look at him, she knew she was in love with him. She supposed Captain Warren was right, that it had begun with their very first meeting, but she could no longer deceive herself about it.

For a while neither spoke. The silence grew pressing. She knew she must get away before it was too late. She left the rail, meaning to go below, but he moved too, and somehow his arms were around her.

'No,' she said, but he knew she did not mean it. She tried to pull away from him but he knew she did not mean that either, and he drew her closer and kissed her.

'No,' she said again, 'we mustn't. We can't let this happen.'

'It has happened. I'm in love with you and you are in love with me.'

'I was never going to tell you that.'

'I knew that. But you don't have to talk.'

Now that it had begun, it was as if all the things they had not said before were saying themselves. 'I knew that first morning, on this very boat, when you looked at me,' she said.

'I loved you before that,' he whispered. 'I loved you in my dreams.'

They stood in the shadows. She could hear the steady throb of the engine and feel the motion of the boat beneath her feet. In the jungle nearby, some tropical bird laughed.

She said, 'Oh, Karl, we can't do this. You can't just go down there tonight and tell Kitty you love me. I think it would destroy her. You don't know how she is about you.'

He smiled faintly. 'Oh yes, I know exactly how she is.'

'And how can I face her after this? I can't go back to Manalos.'

'It doesn't make any difference where you go. I'll find you and come to be with you.'

'No,' she said fiercely, 'I can't do that.'

'And I'm to let you walk off this boat in Belem and forget you exist? That's what you want?'

'Yes. That's what you must do. That's what I want.'

'You're lying,' he said, and kissed her again — not a gentle, affectionate kiss this time but one that was hard and demanding.

They heard voices on the deck below, coming closer, approaching the stairs that led upward. Karl ended the kiss but he did not try to move.

It was she who freed herself from his embrace and turned away from him again, toward the rail. A moment later, Kitty and Clark and Mr. Adams appeared at the top of the stairs.

'There she is,' Kitty said. 'Didn't I tell you she would still be up here looking at the stars? She has a very romantic heart.'

She started across the deck and for the first time saw Karl standing near

127

Elizabeth in the shadows. She stopped, staring from one to the other.

Elizabeth said tremulously, 'Were you looking for me? I'm sorry, I was just coming down and Captain Drayton came along. We stopped to talk about the jungle.'

Kitty said nothing. Mr. Adams asked Karl some question about their progress and Clark made a joke, and the awkward moment was over. For once Elizabeth was glad that Clark was there. He filled the empty silence with a very rapid flow of conversation, and after a few minutes Karl excused himself and left them.

They went below, Mr. Adams and Clark talking a great deal, and joined Mrs. Wilson.

'There, you did find her,' she greeted them. She said to Elizabeth, 'We had just about made up our minds that you slipped off somewhere with that young clerk who was admiring you earlier.'

'Was there a young clerk admiring me?' Elizabeth asked.

'I hate to spoil your notions of romance,' Kitty said, 'but that young clerk is married.'

Mrs. Wilson said, 'I'm always reading about somebody running off with somebody's husband. I don't think anyone cares these days.'

'I expect the wife cares,' Mr. Adams said.

'Maybe not,' Clark said. 'Maybe the wives are happy to be rid of them.'

Mrs. Wilson looked shocked. 'We'd never think such a thing of our husbands, would we, Kitty?'

'I wouldn't,' Kitty said. She sat down beside Mrs. Wilson. In the yellow lamplight her eyes looked like the eyes of a cat. 'I would never let Karl go, no matter what.'

'In the make-believe world of the theater,' Clark said, 'wives murder their husbands for that kind of behavior.'

'That's not just make-believe,' Kitty said. 'I believe I would murder any woman who tried to take my husband away from me.'

Elizabeth shuddered. Kitty had made her remark with such emphasis, it was impossible not to think she meant it.

8

Rio de Janeiro, the River of January, appeared under the right wing of the airplane as they came down through the clouds. The plane dropped downward, and Elizabeth caught glimpses of the curving beaches that edged the city.

Rio was hot and crowded and noisy. Carnival was already in full swing. Even at this early hour the streets were thronged.

Karl had not come with them but had stayed with the *Fair Lady* for the return trip up the river. Elizabeth trailed along after Kitty and Clark. Kitty seemed to have recovered her good spirits completely. Whatever her feelings had been when she had come upon Elizabeth and Karl together on the boat deck, she seemed to have forgotten the entire incident.

'In the old days,' Kitty said, 'the Deodoras kept an apartment here in Rio, just for Carnival time. Now I'm afraid we'll have to settle for a hotel suite.'

Notwithstanding, the hotel to which the cab drove them was luxurious. The suite Kitty had rented was vast and elegant, furnished in French period furniture. A sitting room separated two bedrooms, one for Kitty and one for Elizabeth, each with its own bath.

'I'm afraid you get an ordinary room of your own,' Kitty told Clark, 'but it's just across the hallway.'

They had no sooner deposited their bags in their room than Kitty said, 'I think we should get out into the streets and see some of the goings-on.'

'Yes, of course,' Elizabeth agreed. She had been looking around the expensive suite, thinking of the cost to Kitty. Yet for all her wealth, when it came to love, Kitty Drayton was a pauper.

And, Elizabeth thought, going into her own splendid bedroom with its vast canopied bed and its Empire dressing table, *whatever heartache it costs me, I myself am rich in one thing — Karl's love*.

It would remain a priceless treasure to cherish all her life. For she had made up her mind that they could not be together. After the other evening on the boat, she knew she was not strong enough to risk being around Karl even casually. She had been warned, too, of how ruthless Kitty could be. She had made up her mind that she must find a way to leave Manalos, to avoid tragedy.

She and Kitty left the suite together. 'Aren't we going to stop for Clark?' Elizabeth asked.

'Oh, don't worry about Clark. He'll catch up to us in good time.'

Elizabeth could not help but wonder how anyone could find anyone else in the city, but she offered no objection. On the trip down the river she'd made a point of observing Clark and Kitty together. It was apparent that Clark was completely under Kitty's thumb. Sometimes Kitty was sweet to him and sometimes condescending, and at others she gave him curt orders as if he were a house servant.

It was not difficult to understand their relationship. Clark was an ambitious if only mildly talented actor, stuck in a provincial theater. Kitty, with her obvious fondness for him, her wealth and her tendency to do impulsive things, must seem to him like the one road open to advancement in his life. And if Ruth's information were correct, he had already been named in Kitty's will. Men of more character than Mr. Bennet had been influenced in that manner. She could only wonder how far Clark would be willing to go to keep Kitty happy.

Carnival season was a time when the entire city exploded in an orgy of merrymaking, a period of mass abandon. Brilliant flowers adorned the lamp-posts, and street signs were garlanded with ribbons. Special stands had been erected for the spectators to watch the evening's parades, and klieg lights stood ready to turn night into day.

Already loudspeakers strung up along the streets were blaring out music with the strong samba beat. Kitty and Elizabeth moved along the increasingly crowded street.

★　★　★

Because they had been invited to one of the numerous private balls being held throughout the city, they dined early in the hotel's dining room.

'If we don't go early,' Kitty explained, 'we'll never get there. By seven the streets will be so jammed that the taxis just give up altogether and stop running.'

There had been little time for Elizabeth to plan a costume, but fortunately Ruth Edwards had one from an earlier trip she had made to Carnival and with only minor alterations it fit Elizabeth well. When she came into the sitting room of their hotel suite a short time later, it was as an American southern belle, replete with multitudes of petticoats and a brightly striped parasol that she twirled over one shoulder.

'Well, Scarlett O'Hara, as I live and breathe,' Kitty exclaimed. 'Every man in Rio is going to lose his heart to you or I don't know a thing about anything.'

'Thank you, but you look so beautiful yourself I doubt that anyone will notice me.'

'Oh, this old thing,' Kitty said deprecatingly, but in fact she did look stunning.

She had costumed herself as a lady from the court of Louis XV. Her hair was hidden under an elaborate powdered headdress and her gown of pale blue satin looked authentic down to the last detail. An enormous necklace of diamonds and amethysts, looking equally authentic, lay on her exposed bosom.

'In the old days,' Kitty said wistfully, 'Walter and I never missed a Carnival. One time he came dressed as Louis himself and you've never seen a more splendid monarch.'

She was interrupted by a knock at the door. 'That's Clark,' Kitty said. 'Let him in, will you?'

Elizabeth opened the door and gave an involuntary gasp. She had wondered what sort of costume Clark would choose. Since he must have had at his disposal the entire wardrobe of the theater, he would have rather a wide selection to choose from.

Like Kitty, Clark had dressed in the costume of the court of Louis XV, but he had carried it further. The hands that stretched out toward her now in mock invitation to an embrace were the hands of a skeleton, white cleverly painted upon black, so that in all but the brightest light the illusion was frighteningly real.

Beneath his powdered wig he had painted a skeleton face. At a glance one might think he was dressed as nothing more than a rich-looking French courtier, but when he grinned at you, you found yourself face-to-face with the Prince of Death.

'You don't seem to like my choice of costume,' Clark said, coming into the room.

'It — it's a bit startling,' Elizabeth said, recovering her composure.

'That?' Kitty seemed surprised at Elizabeth's reaction. 'Heavens, I've been scolding Clark for being so unoriginal. If you'll pardon my joke, that idea's been done to death at Carnival. You'll see a thousand skeletons tonight.'

'I suppose it was just that it was so unexpected,' Elizabeth said. 'Even knowing it's you under that makeup I'd have a hard time recognizing you.'

'That's part of the idea, isn't it?' he

said. 'Come on — if we mean to get to the ball before the streets become impassable, we'd better hurry.'

They left word at the desk where they would be if anyone was looking for them, and came out to find the streets almost solid with people. At Kitty's instructions, Clark had arranged for a car and driver and it was waiting just outside, but already it was nearly impossible to get through the mob and they were able to move at no more than a snail's pace.

Watching the crowds from the car's window, Elizabeth saw that Kitty had been right. Both the Louis XV costumes and the skeleton were very common among the Carnival-goers. But although she saw dozens of variations on the Death-figure, none of them struck the cold chill in her heart that the sight of Clark in the hotel doorway had. She could not understand why a handsome and obviously vain man like Clark should have chosen to hide his face beneath that grotesque makeup.

Finally, after what seemed hours of driving, they arrived at the hillside mansion at which the ball was being held. Their hosts, according to Kitty, were among the city's elite. Although the old Empire was long since gone from Brazil, the aristocratic past lingered on here in Rio just as it did in Manalos. There were two pretenders to the non-existent imperial throne, both of them well-known society figures, and there remained families like their hosts for this ball who still valued large landed estates more highly than new fortunes. In the midst of poverty and exploitation, the country's aristocrats maintained their traditions of polished elegance.

This ball and others like it throughout the city were part of that old elegance and the elite was out in full force. Besides the costumed masqueraders there were scores of men in full military costume, and others in conventional formal attire.

Kitty seemed to know everyone. After a few minutes Elizabeth's head was spinning from introductions and when she found herself separated from Kitty by the crowd, she did not attempt to regain her side but drifted off on her own.

Elizabeth saw Clark a short time later, in conversation with two men in clown costumes and two in ordinary street clothes. She might not have noticed them at all, but the two in street clothes struck a jarring note. They did not seem to belong to this gracious setting, and had the air of men not accustomed to such luxury. They looked, more than anything else, like movie gangsters, and she wondered what on earth Clark could have to discuss with them. She reminded herself that he had lived here in Rio, and probably not always in luxury; and Brazil was unique in that sense, that men who were construction workers or jungle fighters could overnight acquire great wealth and afterward mingle with the upper crust.

In time she found herself seated at a small table by the dance floor, sharing it with an American woman whose name she hadn't caught and who seemed quite dazzled by all the uproar.

'Isn't this grand?' she exclaimed. 'It must have cost a fortune. Oh, what a handsome man. Why, he's coming this way.'

Instinctively, Elizabeth knew who she would see when she looked in that direction, and her heart stopped beating.

Karl came directly to her table, stopping and giving her a little bow. The American woman was thrilled and fanned herself energetically, obviously hoping for an introduction.

'Hello,' Elizabeth greeted him lamely. 'I don't know just where Kitty is. Have you seen her?'

'No. I want to talk to you.'

She knew she should refuse. If Kitty saw him and realized he had come to her before even looking for his own wife, there would certainly be trouble.

'Excuse me, please,' she said to the disappointed American. A few feet away French doors opened onto a tiled terrace, dimly lit. Her cheeks hot, she led the way outside. The night breeze ruffled her hair.

Once outside she turned to face him. She wanted desperately to fling herself into his arms but she restrained herself.

'What are you doing here?' she asked.

'I had to come.' His face looked bleak in the light of the flaring torch nearby.

'We had some trouble with the boat. Nothing major, but it meant waiting there in Belem another day. I sat in a damned hotel room and told myself I would only come to see some of the Carnival, and I wouldn't come near you while I was here. It didn't do any good. As soon as I got off the plane I came straight to the hotel. They told me at the desk where to find you.'

They stood for a moment just looking at one another. It was like trying to discuss intimate personal affairs before a vast audience. All around them was the sound of music and bands playing the samba, and people passing jostled them.

'We can't talk like this,' he said, casting an annoyed glance around. 'Come on, there's a garden here.'

She went with him down stone steps that led to a small garden, with some potted shrubs and a little bench, all of it under the canopy of a great palm tree.

In the shadow of the palm tree, he put his arm about her.

'No,' she said, 'someone might come.'

'No one will see. It's dark.'

'They might. We can't take that risk. You don't know what it might mean.'

'The only thing I care about is you.'

'That isn't true. You care about your boats, for one thing. Don't you see? If Kitty ever found out about us, you would lose everything. You would have me about your neck like a great stone, and nothing else.'

'Without you there is nothing else.' He put his arms about her again and this time she let him kiss her. 'Now will you believe me?' he asked, taking his lips from hers.

'I believe you love me, and I love you too. That's why I can't let you ruin everything for yourself.'

'There is nothing to ruin.' He tried to kiss her again. There was a light sound of laughter just beyond the stone steps. She turned her face away quickly.

He let her go as suddenly as he had seized her. 'Is that all this means to you?' he demanded hotly. 'Someone might see us? Someone might know how we feel?'

'But I told you . . . '

'I've told you nothing matters. Are you

waiting for me to ask you to marry me? What did you think I came here for, to wrestle for a few minutes in the darkness? Or did you think I meant for you to check into some hotel room with me for the night? Don't be a fool. I'll tell Kitty I want to be free and then I mean for us to be married.'

She felt as if a great weight were pressing down upon her. 'I can't accept that. I decided that the other night on the *Fair Lady*. I will make inquiries. I decided I would never see you again. I'm not going back to Manalos.'

'You're lying,' he said. 'You are alone too. It's the two of us against the world. You can't go back to that any more than I could.'

'Why, good heavens, it's Karl. Hello.' It was Clark's voice from the top of the steps. So rapt were they in one another, neither Elizabeth nor Karl had heard him approach.

Kitty appeared beyond Clark's shoulder and said, with one of her too-bright smiles, 'I thought I saw you come in.'

Elizabeth put a foot on the steps. 'We

were looking for you,' she lied.

Kitty came down the steps into the little garden. She was trying to keep up appearances and Elizabeth wished she could help her but she simply hadn't the will to pretend.

Kitty swept by her without a glance and came directly to Karl, laying on hand on his arm. 'I'm so thrilled you could make it after all,' she said. 'What a wonderful surprise, your coming all this way just to see me.'

'I have to go back,' he said curtly, no pretense in his voice or his manner. 'I left the boat at Belem. I remembered something I hadn't told Miss Parker.'

Kitty did look at her then and despite the smile the look in her eyes was murderous. 'My, it must have been something very important to bring you flying down here just to tell her. Tell me, Liz, darling, what is this dark secret you two have cooked up between you? I'll bet it's about my birthday, isn't it?'

Elizabeth could say nothing. She looked from Karl to Kitty and to Clark, the Death face grinning wickedly. She felt that she had to get away, must be somewhere by herself where she could think and sort out her swirling emotions.

'Excuse me,' she said, and ran up the steps to the terrace. She pushed her way through the crowds, toward the front door. A liveried servant stood just inside the door, but when she asked him about a taxi he looked at her as if she were mad.

'It is Carnival,' he said, shaking his head. 'No cars will be running until morning.'

'But how can I get back to my hotel?'

'You can walk,' he said, as if he did not quite believe her capable of that feat. He pointed. 'That street will lead you to Floriano Square.'

Fortunately the dense crowds were moving, seemingly all of the thousands and thousands of people heading as she was for Floriano Square. Occasionally she would find herself seized and danced along with one of the samba groups, and from time to time one of the ornate floats inched its way through the mobs. One young man in a pirate costume grabbed her by the waist and twirled her around.

'Stay with me, beautiful lady,' he cried over the din of music and shouting voices, but in the next moment the crowd had separated them and swept him away. She had a last glimpse of him laughing wildly, quite unconcerned at losing his partner of the moment.

At last she reached the square. She was sucked into a world-gone-mad frenzy of people drinking from bottles, throwing confetti, tooting horns and spraying perfume. She was embraced and twirled about and in a moment she had lost all sense of direction.

'Please,' she cried when someone held her arm and tried to pull her along with him. He let her go and another man tried to kiss her. She screamed and the crowd dragged him away.

'Dearie, it's terrible,' a lady beside her shouted. 'Someone's going to get trampled to death before this is over.'

She stumbled backward and was shoved forward again, and she fell to her knees. She heard her skirt tear and for a horrible moment she thought she actually might be trampled to death. It was like a nightmare, all these shoving, milling people. This was no longer a festival, but a horror in which she was trapped.

Someone grabbed her roughly, jerking her to her feet, and she saw a familiar Death face, but now it was a welcome sight.

'Clark,' she said, trying to thank him, but conversation was impossible. He led her through the crowds, forcing a path for them. She followed gladly, stumbling along in his wake.

He drew her into a doorway, holding her in front of him and shielding her from the crowd with his own body. She leaned back against him gratefully. His arms closed about her and she gave a gasp of relief.

'Thank God you found me,' she said.

'Yes. Or thank the devil,' he replied. His voice was so strange, so strangled-sounding, that it gave her an eerie feeling. Before her was a darkened window in which she could dimly see their reflections. He held her tightly and grinned over her shoulder at their ghostly images in the glass.

He reached around her and rattled the handle of the door. It opened and he pulled her inside. They were in a dark hallway, the air warm and sour-smelling. The sound of the Cariocas outside was muted here.

He turned her roughly about and kissed her, his lips hard and demanding on hers. She struggled against him, twisting her face away.

'Clark,' she said, her voice rising. His grip on her arm was rough, actually hurting her now. A sudden thought leapt into her consciousness. 'You are Clark, aren't you?' she asked, trying to see his face in the gloom of the hall. For an answer he only laughed and tried again to kiss her.

Panic swept over her. She had thought it was Clark — the Death face, the French costume. But there were so many men dressed the same way. What if this wasn't Clark?

'Please,' she said, in the grip of fear, 'who are you?'

'Death,' he whispered.

One arm held her fast and the free

hand went to her throat. She tried to scream but the hand tightened violently and her scream came out only a hoarse, choking sound.

9

A door crashed open on the landing above them, banging back against the wall, and the hall was flooded with light from within the apartment. There was an explosion of sound and scent and light and the hall was suddenly filled with people spilling out of a party.

Elizabeth was swept out of his arms before she or he quite realized what was happening. She had a glimpse of three laughing senhoritas surrounding him, trying to kiss and embrace him, and then she was through the door and outside, gulping the hot air gratefully.

She plunged into the mob on the street, only to find it more jam-packed than before. She was glad for one thing — surely no one could trail her through this.

Someone suddenly pushed her off balance and she would have fallen if the crowd hadn't been too thick-packed to prevent that. A group of street revelers singing and dancing together shoved its way through. They snaked past her and she saw, at the end of the group, a grinning skeleton.

With a little cry of fear she elbowed past the people in front of her. An alleyway opened off the square just a few feet away. In another moment she was out of the crowd, in the narrow passageway between two buildings, and she began to run, gasping for breath. Behind her someone shouted, but whether it was the skeleton or only some merrymaker she didn't know and she did not look back to see.

Another alley intersected this one and she turned to her right and ran down that one, so dark she could hardly see where she was going. Another turning, and ahead, light reflected dimly from a shaded window, revealing a shadowy doorway practically beside her. She stepped into it, breathing heavily, and leaned against the rough brick. In the distance she heard the sound of running footsteps. They paused and she could imagine her pursuer listening, looking up and down the alleys, wondering.

The steps ran again, fading into the

distance. She was alone. She remained where she was for several minutes, until her breathing had returned to normal, and with it came a sense of foolishness at her panic. A strange man whom she had mistaken for Clark had helped her out of the crowd and as a reward had tried to make love to her. And he had jokingly attempted to frighten her into submitting to his desires. That was all that had happened, and she had gotten out of it with no real harm done.

Smiling into the darkness at her own silliness, she stepped from the doorway and started along the alley. She came around a corner and a second one, and stopped. A short distance ahead a wrought-iron fence blocked the alley and made of its ending a private patio with a walkway leading toward the square.

And in the walkway, his back to her, stood a cloaked figure.

She tried to step back around the corner, unseen, but her sudden appearance had startled an alley cat feeding from a garbage can. He gave a yowl and leaped for the fence, rattling the metal can.

The man across the patio turned, his cape swirling, and she saw a skeleton face and the satin gleam of a French costume. In an instant he was racing across the little patio, leaping at the fence. She saw him scrambling up and at last she overcame the terror that held her there and, with a strangled cry, she turned and ran.

She reached the doorway in which she had sheltered before and darted into it, pressing herself into the shadows. She held her breath, and it was like a fire in her breast, burning with agonizing intensity.

Someone ran past in a flurry of movement, cape billowing after him. It lasted no more than a second, and he was gone. She fought against the scream that rose in her throat. Behind her something moved and her heart ceased its pounding for a full second.

It was only the door she had been leaning against, swinging inward. She did not hesitate but stepped inside, closing it behind her.

She was in another apartment building,

153

the corridor stretching straight before her to the front entrance. That was open, too, and she could see the crowded square beyond.

She stepped out into the busy square again. She found that she was near one of the huge grandstands that had been set up for viewing the parade. If she could get to that she would be at the elbows, as it were, of numerous officials and policemen. Surely she would be safe there until she could think how to reach the hotel.

Slowly but insistently she pushed her way through the throngs of people, toward the metal rails of the grandstand. A somewhat inebriated but gallant gentleman helped her the last few feet, making a path for her and actually handing her into a grandstand seat.

A group of military officers sat just a few feet away. One of them cast an approving eye in her direction. Yes, she would be safe here, and when she had rested for a bit and gotten her bearings she would try again to reach the hotel. Perhaps one of those officers would even accompany her, and who would dare to molest her then?

Now that she had successfully escaped from him, she could think more clearly about the skeleton who had pursued her. He had seemed so like Clark, but there was no reason for Clark to have treated her with such cruelty or to try to frighten her.

Or was that true? He was completely under Kitty's thumb. Would Kitty have gone so far as to order him to follow her, frighten her badly or even harm her? And if she did, would Clark have done as she ordered?

She looked around the square, gradually getting her sense of direction back. Yes, if she crossed the square and went down that street over there, she would be back at the hotel. Not so far after all, although she did not relish the prospect of fighting her way across the square.

The people around her began to laugh and a great noise of squealing and shouting erupted. Another float was inching its way into the area in front of the grandstand, this one filled with a group of clowns.

For a moment she had an odd queasy

feeling — at a glance, two of the clowns on the float looked like the ones she had seen Clark talking to earlier at the ball. She gave her head a shake and told herself she was becoming paranoid.

Yet . . . several times as the float moved at its snail's pace, she thought one or the other of the painted men glanced in her direction. She could not quite rid herself of the impression that they were looking for her.

Two of the clowns, Harlequin and Columbine, were clearly crowd favorites. The float featured a house of sorts with make-do doors and windows, and the essence of their charade was familiar and obviously well-loved nonsense. Having been spurned by a haughty Columbine, Harlequin meant to abduct her from under the nose of her highly suspicious guardian, who kept wandering in and out of the 'house' in a nightshirt, brandishing a large club.

Harlequin's own 'club', hidden inside his blouse, proved to be a string of sausages, and the figure he abducted from the bed was not Columbine after all, but her father, chewing on an oversized cigar. The audience roared with delight as Columbine ran round and round the float, pursued by Harlequin who was in turn pursued by the clown in the nightshirt.

On the float, now almost directly in front of Elizabeth, Columbine had disappeared through a trapdoor and everyone — Harlequin, Papa and diverse others — was hunting for her. They ran around the float calling, 'Columbine! Where's Columbine?'

'How can I marry without a bride?' Harlequin cried in English and again in Portuguese. Elizabeth laughed with the crowd.

One of the clowns suddenly shouted, 'Look, there's Sophia, she will be your bride.' He pointed into the grandstand, pretending to recognize someone.

'Sophia, Sophia,' Harlequin cried in impassioned delight. 'Yes, I will marry Sophia.'

He sprang down from the barely moving float to the street and ran toward the grandstand. The others jumped down too and followed behind him. 'Sophia,' they all shouted.

They were running directly toward Elizabeth. The crowd, which had been a solid wall of watchers before, melted aside to form a path for them, everyone eager to see what was to come next.

Elizabeth had a sudden sense of what was happening and half-rose from her seat, crying, 'No!'

Her cry was swallowed up in a roar of laughter as the clowns reached her and seized her in their arms, lifting her bodily from the grandstand and carrying her back to the float, where she was dumped unceremoniously onto the floor of the float.

'Sophia,' the clowns continued to shout. Laughing, they danced and pushed one another around her, forming a ring. She tried to get up and slipped and fell, and the audience screamed with laughter.

Elizabeth was overcome with horror at the nightmare situation. She was being mauled and thrown about, kidnapped before the eyes of thousands of spectators, and she saw how she looked to them, not terrified and desperate, but comical. A real kidnapping, a comic marriage abduction — where did humor end and horror take over? Now she knew.

She tried to break away from her captors and run, but someone or something tripped her and she fell into a pile of sawdust, to a roar of delight from the audience. Someone struck her, knocking the breath out of her, but even if she had been able to scream, her protests would have been lost in the pandemonium. She was lifted by her hands and feet and swung wildly around, until the world was a spinning blur.

They began to toss her into the air, catching her and tossing her again. Her limbs felt disjointed, flopping ridiculously with each toss. It was the stuff of haunted dreams — the shouting, the jangle of the music from the loudspeakers, the tossing into the air and falling back again — a mad, desperate montage of horrible sensations. She saw Harlequin's face, painted with great streaks of blue and red, his hat cocked to one side. He was laughing grotesquely.

The laughter had begun to fade slightly and she realized that the float had moved past the grandstand. They had truly taken her away before all those watching eyes. She had been kidnapped with thousands of witnesses all laughing at her plight.

They dropped her heavily to the floor of the float and rolled her over and over in a canvas sheet, wrapped like a cocoon with only her legs and feet protruding from one end. Blackness enveloped her and she felt half-smothered and sick. She was lifted and flung across someone's shoulder. Nearby a door opened on noisy hinges.

She realized in a flash that they were taking her inside the float, out of sight altogether, and as horrible as the ordeal had been thus far, she could not even bear to think what more they had in store for her.

'Hurry, bring her in here,' someone said in a loud whisper.

The sheet that held her was tight around her head and shoulders, but she could still move her feet at least. She was over the shoulder of one of the clowns, her head dangling down his back. He smelled of sweat and greasepaint and cigar smoke, making her want to retch.

She kicked with all the strength she could find in her legs, right into his crotch. For an instant the man just froze, as if turned to stone. They he gave a great bleat of pain, staggered, and fell, dropping her.

She rolled, the sheet unwinding, and suddenly she was free again, scrambling to her knees at the edge of the float. Someone grabbed her legs to prevent her escape. She was right in the crowd now, laughing faces only a few feet from her own.

'Help me,' she cried in despair. 'For God's sake, someone help me!'

The faces vanished as the sheet of canvas was tossed over her again and a second later someone had fallen across her, knocking the breath from her again. She kicked and fought, blinded by the canvas and weak with exhaustion and frustration. Miraculously the weight was suddenly gone.

Someone grabbed her arms, lifting her

to her feet, and she kicked out savagely again.

'Hey, easy there,' a masculine voice said beside her in what was obviously American English.

A moment later the canvas was whisked away and she could breathe — and see. What she saw were three worried faces and the olive drab of American Marine uniforms. Another Marine was behind her, lifting her up.

'Are you okay?' the young man directly in front of her asked.

For an answer she began to cry. She let herself sink back into the arms of the man behind her.

'I told you that was no act,' one of the Marines said. 'I said she looked scared to death, didn't I?'

'Those dirty bastards,' one of them swore, but the clowns had already vanished from the float, jumping down and disappearing into the mob. And already Elizabeth saw that the crowd had lost interest in her. A few curious faces were still turned in her direction, but for the most part the drama that had nearly cost her so dearly had ceased to amuse them. The comedy was over and they had turned to other, more interesting spectacles.

The Marines lifted her down from the float. Sobbing, she managed to tell them where she wanted to go and, with their escort, she was taken swiftly through the crowds, straight across the square. She wondered at the ease with which they made a path through the dense crowd. In no more than minutes they had delivered her to the door of her hotel.

She paused at the steps to look at her rescuers — fresh-faced young men, no longer boys and not quite yet men.

She kissed each of them lightly and they disappeared into the crowd, laughing and talking.

She looked very much disheveled as she came through the hotel's lobby, but the staff apparently were used to that at Carnival and hardly anyone gave her a second glance.

By the time she reached the hotel suite, reaction had begun to set in. She paused in the hallway outside feeling suddenly quite weak in the knees. Memory of the nightmarish scene with the clowns on the float flooded back in on her and she was barely able to open the door for the trembling of her hands.

Kitty was in the sitting room, drinking a cup of tea. She looked up, startled, as Elizabeth came in. 'Liz! What on earth happened to you?'

'Not nearly so much as might have happened,' Elizabeth said. 'Is there more of that tea?'

'Yes, yes, certainly. Here, let me pour you a cup and you sit down and tell me everything.'

Kitty fussed and clucked, pouring tea. It was hard for Elizabeth to imagine now that Kitty might have wished her any harm.

Elizabeth told her story chronologically, and although she did not explain why she thought Clark might have been the man in the skeleton costume, she did say, 'He looked so much like Clark that even after everything happened I still couldn't be sure it wasn't.'

'But, darling, in the first place, Clark would be the last person to want to hurt you. Why, you know as well as I do, he's crazy about you. And in the second place, he's been back here for ages. Wait, let me get him for you. I wouldn't for a minute let you think Clark had done anything like that.'

She went out, determined to produce Clark for Elizabeth's inspection. For her own part, Elizabeth would have preferred to see Karl or ask what had happened to him, since he was nowhere in evidence here, but she was afraid of the reaction that question might produce. And it was just as well he wasn't here, she told herself. How could she have helped throwing herself into his arms?

In less than a minute Kitty was back with Clark in tow. He was wearing a dressing gown and there was no trace of the previous makeup or costume.

'What's this about your thinking I was trying to scare you?' he asked, grinning.

'It was just that someone with a similar costume and makeup did give me a scare,' Elizabeth said. 'And I think if I hadn't been lucky, there'd have been much worse than that before it was over.'

At Kitty's insistence, Elizabeth had to tell her story again while Clark listened. He seemed to be hearing it for the first time and he looked, as the story went along, genuinely upset. But then, she reminded herself, he was an actor, and he would have had plenty of time to get back to the hotel and very quickly remove costume and makeup.

She said nothing about thinking the clowns who tried to abduct her might have been the same ones she had seen him talking to at the ball.

When she had finished her story, Clark said, 'We'd better report all this to the police.'

Kitty looked dismayed by the prospect. 'But what on earth for?' she asked. 'How do you think they're going to find a man in a skeleton costume, or a group of clowns, in that commotion out there? And think of the scandal.'

'But think of what almost happened,' he said.

'Please,' Elizabeth said, 'Kitty's right. Aside from a bad scare and some bumps and bruises, I haven't suffered anything.

166

And there's little likelihood of ever finding the men involved. Even if they did find them, I wouldn't be able to identify them, don't you see? No, I think I would just as soon try to forget this whole business.'

'Yes, and I'm going to send you straight home tomorrow,' Kitty said in a brook-no-argument voice. 'I can't have you making that long trip back on the boat. The best thing for you is to get straight back to Manalos and you'll have plenty of time to rest and recover before school opens again. There's a little charter airline that flies to the interior cities. I'm going to send you home with them. You remember that outfit, don't you, Clark?'

'Yes, I took one of their planes back the last time. It's a lot quicker and easier than the other way,' he said, directing this last at Elizabeth, who still looked doubtful.

'There, you see, it's all settled,' Kitty said, steering Elizabeth firmly toward her bedroom. 'Now don't you worry about a thing. You just get some sleep and Clark and I will make all the necessary arrangements.'

10

Elizabeth woke to a knocking at her bedroom door. She went to open it, expecting to find Kitty there, the arrangements all satisfactorily made for her to fly back to Manalos. To her surprise, she found Karl at her door instead.

'They've told me what happened to you yesterday,' he said. 'I've come to take you away from here.'

'And you've wasted a trip,' Kitty said from just behind him. 'I've already arranged a charter flight for her. The plane leaves at . . . '

'You can cancel it. She'll go back on the boat — where I can see that she's safe.'

'But that little charter service has a perfect safety record. And she'll be home so much quicker that way,' Kitty argued.

Karl seemed not to have heard her. 'Will it take you long to pack?' he asked Elizabeth.

She hesitated. She knew that if she accepted his offer, she was crossing the Rubicon, making a decision that could not be unmade. Kitty would never forgive her — and she could not pretend again that there was nothing between herself and Karl.

'Only a few minutes,' she answered his question.

When they left together, Kitty did not even say goodbye or wish her well. She stood in the middle of the sitting room and glowered at them as they went.

★ ★ ★

'Where are we going?' she asked when they were in a cab, rushing through the streets of Rio.

'To my hotel,' he said.

She went silent for a moment. He seemed to sense a momentary uncertainty in her and drew her to him and kissed her.

'You needn't be afraid,' he said. 'And we needn't . . . well, I do have to pick up my things. If you'd be more comfortable

169

waiting downstairs . . . '

'No. I'm not afraid,' she said. 'Just, tell me, please, you won't ever be sorry.'

'Me, sorry? Don't be ridiculous. Without you there's never been anything for me but one form of hell or another.' He held her in a long embrace.

'And afterward?' she asked finally.

'I don't know,' he said. 'I'm still sorting it all out. We'll have to go back to Manalos, to face Kitty. I want a divorce. She'll put up a terrible stink, but I want to be able to marry you. I don't want anything less than that. But don't expect Kitty to let go easily. She's not the sort to let go of anything she regards as hers.'

'It doesn't matter, as long as we can be together,' she said.

'It matters to me,' Karl said. 'I want us to be married.'

She shrugged. 'I don't care what people say. I used to, but not now.'

If there were a scandal, if people talked, what difference would it make? In twenty, thirty years, who would remember, or care? Time moved on, life followed its own course, and yesterday's tragedies mattered no more than yesterday's trivialities.

He kissed her again, holding her close to him until the cab driver, with a polite cough, informed them they were at the hotel.

* * *

From the hotel, much later, they went directly to the airport where they caught a flight to Belem. Captain Warren and the *Fair Lady* were waiting for them there to make the return trip to Manalos.

She was given the cabin that had been Kitty's before. It was the boat's finest cabin and was used by dignitaries or by the captain's wife.

'I haven't any right to this,' she said, looking around at the elegant furnishings.

'I don't know anyone who has more right,' Karl said.

A black man came with a tray and some cold supper, compliments of Captain Warren. The captain had been subdued when he saw Elizabeth, only welcoming her aboard, but she thought from the twinkle in his eye that he knew things had changed between her and Karl and was rather more pleased than not.

When the waiter had gone, she came and sat at the little table that had been set up for them. Karl poured her a glass of wine and she sipped it gratefully.

'This is our first meal together,' she said. 'Our first meal alone.'

'There will be others. A lifetime of them.'

*   *   *

She was aware as she came off the boat with Karl in Manalos that she was the object of many stares. She was sure, too, that many people were taking note of the way in which Karl took her arm as he helped her onto the landing.

By now, they knew that Kitty was back in Manalos, having taken the very charter airplane she had recommended for Elizabeth. Karl did not take her to the Bishop's Palace, however, but to one of the hotels downtown, the El Dorado.

'I think if you're going to talk about us,

I should be there with you when you see Kitty,' she had said, but he had decided otherwise.

'There's no telling what Kitty might say or do. Murder wouldn't surprise me. I want you safe away from her and that house.'

So she waited in the hotel room, while he went to the Bishop's Palace to tell his wife what she surely already knew, that he was in love with another woman. The time passed slowly.

She stood at the window for a while, watching the people passing by below. She felt sure that, by the next day, her name would be on everyone's tongue and she had no doubt that most of them would sympathize with Kitty. She was the wronged wife, and Elizabeth the interloper. What could any of them know about the needs or frustrations that had brought all this to pass?

She had checked into the hotel late in the morning and by mid-afternoon she felt she could no longer endure pacing to and fro in the increasingly suffocating room. She went down to the lobby and, leaving word at the desk where she would be, she had coffee in the little lunch room there.

She sat for nearly an hour, sipping the strong black coffee. She was about to leave and return to her room when she saw Karl coming through the lobby. He stopped at the front desk and then came directly toward the lunch room.

Her eyes searched his face as he sat down. Her hands were trembling and, so that he would not see, she put them in her lap.

'It's all right,' he said, wasting no time on preamble. 'She's going to give me a divorce.'

'She . . . ' She could hardly believe her ears. 'Is she? But what did she say? Darling, you've been hours. Tell me what happened.'

'We talked business most of the time. I told her first off that I was in love with you, that I wanted a divorce so that I could marry you, and that it didn't make any difference what she did. If she wouldn't divorce me, I would leave with you anyway, and she'd have that scandal to live with. Surprisingly enough, she took it very calmly. She said she had known, of course, that we were in love, and had just been waiting for me to bring the subject into the open.'

'And that was all?' Elizabeth felt a bit dazed.

'It's surprising, isn't it? There was more discussion than that, of course, but as I said, she was completely calm the whole time. She said she had always thought you were a delightful person and if she had to lose me to someone, she couldn't think of anyone she'd prefer. It was a very sophisticated conversation, really. She even suggested you move back into the palace, but I refused that idea outright.'

'And the business part of it? I don't suppose I will understand it, but after all, something has kept you there all day.'

He grinned. 'Yes, that's the second piece of news. She said she supposed I would like to keep the boat line. I thought she might be looking for some hold to get on me, so I was a little cautious. But what she had in mind was letting me purchase it, at a very reasonable price. As she pointed out, she could hardly run it herself so she would have to sell it in any case, and why not to me? So what we've come up with is, I'm going to fly back down to Rio. There's a man there I think will back me. If he agrees, I'll be free of Kitty and I'll still have the Drayton lines.'

'When do we leave?' Elizabeth asked, and knew at once from the guilty look that flashed across his face that this wasn't what he had in mind. 'You were planning to go without me, weren't you?'

'Well, to tell you the truth, darling, it would be quicker and easier for me to go alone. I can be back in two days, three at the most, and I won't even have to bother with a hotel room; I'll just rough it.'

'But . . . what if Kitty tries to pull any more of her stunts while you're gone?'

'She won't. She knows I'm on to her now, for starters. And you won't be at the palace, you'll be here in the hotel. All you've got to do is sit tight. She's not likely to burst into your room with a gun, or anything drastic like that. Think of what she did before — if she really did those things. She persuaded Bennet to scare you, and those clowns to abduct you, though they might have only been trying to scare you too. Well, she can't control an entire hotel, can she?'

'No, of course not,' she said.

'I understand how you must feel. But it is crucial that I go, and at once, and I can travel faster alone, which means I can be back sooner. And considering how agreeable she's being, I thought it best if I arrange things as promptly as I can, before she changes her mind.'

'I agree with you. I just don't like being away from you. This day seemed like an eternity.' She sighed. 'When will you leave?'

'If I hurry, there's a chance to hop a flight this evening.' He stood and hesitated for a moment, looking down at her. 'You'll be all right, then?'

'Absolutely.'

She watched him stride across the lobby and in a minute he was gone.

She was still a little dazed by the ease with which everything had been resolved. She thought of Kitty on the boat, on their way to Rio, vowing that no one would ever take Karl from her.

Had she changed her mind that simply? Or had Karl been deluded by his own hope into believing something that wasn't true?

11

Later in the afternoon, Ruth Edwards phoned. 'I heard you were back in town,' she said. 'To be honest, people are talking of nothing else. Well, you know how much I care about this town and the people in it. Listen, I've got an idea. Orrin is working tonight; let's have dinner together.'

Elizabeth hesitated. 'I hadn't planned on going out,' she said.

'No need to go anywhere; we can eat right there in the hotel,' Ruth said. 'It's about the only decent restaurant left in town anyway.'

In the face of Ruth's determined friendliness, Elizabeth relented and in less than an hour she joined her in the dining room and they sat down to dinner.

Elizabeth had not been able to shake her feelings of foreboding, of some disaster impending. She simply did not believe in Kitty's generosity of spirit and she wondered when Kitty's true nature would come to the fore again.

She did not have long to wait. She and Ruth had scarcely ordered dinners when a shadow fell over the table and Elizabeth looked up to find Kitty standing there. Her face was absolutely glowing with excitement and anger.

'Well, if it isn't my dear friend, Liz,' she said.

'Kitty, won't you join us, please?' Elizabeth started from her chair.

'Oh no, no, dear friend, don't get up on account of me,' Kitty said, putting a hand claw-like on Elizabeth's shoulder. 'We are dear friends, aren't we? Even if you have tried to steal my husband from me, surely that doesn't stop our being friends, does it?'

'Kitty, for lord's sake,' Ruth said. 'People are staring.'

Kitty turned on her with a flash of anger. 'Shut up. Let them,' she said. 'And you,' she turned back to Elizabeth, 'you slut, you're a fool if you think you'll ever marry Karl Drayton. He's married to me and he will be as long as we both live, and you will never change that.'

'I don't care whether that changes or not,' Elizabeth said. 'I plan to leave Manalos one way or another, and Karl insists he means to come with me, regardless of what you do or don't do. It would be easier, of course, if you agreed to a divorce, as I understood you meant to do, but . . . '

'I never meant to do that,' Kitty said. 'And I never will. I just told him that to give myself time to consider things. But whatever happens, I can tell you one thing for certain: you needn't think you'll leave this city with him. The only way you will ever get him is over my dead body.'

With that she turned and stalked from the room, pushing past a startled waiter and nearly making him drop the tray he carried. She was gone as suddenly as she had appeared. The silence in the dining room lingered in her wake. Elizabeth was aware that the other diners had all been watching the scene avidly.

A different waiter brought their first courses, setting them swiftly and silently before them and hurrying away as if he feared he might become embroiled in their difficulties.

It was Ruth who finally broke the silence. 'I guess if you were still staying up at the palace, you'd be planning how to go about strangling Kitty in her sleep, wouldn't you?'

Elizabeth smiled and said, 'I think poison would be easier. In her tea, maybe.'

She glanced up and saw that Ruth was staring past her. Elizabeth looked over her shoulder and discovered that Maria had come into the dining room. She stood a foot or so away, timidly waiting for an opportunity to approach.

Elizabeth blushed, wondering if Maria had heard their remarks, but Maria's face was as impassive as ever. She came quickly to the table, without offering any greeting or pretending to friendliness. She looked frightened at being there — consorting with the enemy, as Elizabeth supposed she saw it.

'I've had your things packed and brought down here,' Maria said. 'I left them at the desk.'

'That was very kind of you,' Elizabeth said, and added mentally, *and brave*, considering what the mood must have been at the palace since Karl had gone. 'I don't know how to thank you.'

'It isn't necessary.' She bobbed her head and scurried away, looking right and left as if she expected Kitty to pop out from behind a column and upbraid her for being there.

'Well,' Ruth said, spearing a piece of melon, 'dinner with you is far more eventful than with Orrin and Denny.'

Elizabeth said nothing but began to eat in silence, her thoughts far from her food. Karl had been wrong. Kitty had deceived him into believing she would give him up without a fight. But how did Kitty mean to prevent them from leaving Manalos?

What would she do to stop them?

★ ★ ★

Elizabeth determined when she got up the following morning that she would stay right here in her room until Karl returned, later this day or on the next one. Better a day or two of confinement than another clash with Kitty. And at least on that score, Karl had been right — so long as she stayed in the sanctity of her room, there was nothing Kitty could do to her.

It was shortly after lunch that a knock came at the door. For a moment she hesitated to answer it, half-afraid that Kitty had come for another confrontation.

The knock came again, loud and insistent. She opened the door and found two gentlemen there, one in the uniform of the local police and the other in a rather crumpled suit.

'Senhorita Parker?' the man in the suit asked. Elizabeth nodded, her throat so dry she did not trust her voice to speak. Her first thought was of Karl — something had happened to Karl.

'I am Senhor Mendoza of the Manalos civil police,' he introduced himself, 'and this is Captain Lopez. May we come in?'

She opened the door wider and they stepped in, closing the door after themselves. 'Is something wrong?' she asked, 'Has something happened?'

Lopez took up a position by the door and remained silent. Mendoza, who seemed to be in charge, said, ignoring her question, 'You arrived back in Manalos yesterday, Senhorita, that is correct?'

'Yes, that is correct, but . . . '

He gave her no chance to speak but went on smoothly. While he spoke, his eyes continued to look around and around the room, as if searching for something, but she had no idea what it might be.

'You have been here in the hotel, most of the time since your return, is that right?' She nodded, growing increasingly impatient for him to explain. 'And last night, you were visited by Senhora Drayton, were you not?'

Elizabeth stiffened. Something cold touched the base of her spine, like an icy finger. 'She was here briefly, yes. Not here in my room, but downstairs. While I was eating dinner.'

'You had a quarrel, I understand.' For the first time he turned his dark eyes, cold and penetrating, directly upon her. 'A quarrel over Mr. Drayton who, if I understand correctly, planned to leave Manalos and his wife and go away with you.'

'I'm not sure that's anyone's business,'

Elizabeth said sharply. Her mind was racing, trying to think where all this could be leading. She had forgotten she was in an almost forgotten city deep in the Amazon rain forest, and that in this city Kitty was a powerful political force. She did not know what limits the law put on personal vengeance, but it was entirely possible that in some way Kitty meant to use the law against her. Perhaps she even meant to have her arrested on some trumped-up charge. It occurred to her that she did not know the local law at all. If it came to that, she would have to ask Ruth Edwards for help.

Senhor Mendoza ignored her remark. 'Senhora Drayton told you, I believe, that the only way you could leave with Senhor Drayton was over her dead body. That is the phrase she used, is it not?'

'You seem very well informed already,' Elizabeth said coldly. 'But, yes, a number of people overheard our quarrel. It was only a figure of speech, as I'm sure you must know.'

Senhor Mendoza said, 'Ah, but in this instance it has proved to be more than just a figure of speech, would it not seem?'

Elizabeth looked at him blankly. 'I don't understand what you mean,' she said.

He smiled without a trace of cheer. 'Senhora Drayton told you how you could have her husband, and now it has been arranged, just as she suggested.'

For a moment Elizabeth still could not comprehend what he was trying to tell her. 'I don't . . . ' she stammered.

'Or did you not know? Senhora Drayton is dead.'

Elizabeth took a step backward and one hand went to her throat.

'Kitty? Dead? But, how? . . . She was fine yesterday.'

'Yes, so I am told,' Senhor Mendoza replied. 'As to how, she has been murdered. Poisoned.'

The simple word, delivered in a soft, unemotional voice, was like the explosion of a bomb in the little hotel room.

'I — I must sit down,' Elizabeth said, feeling dazed.

The policeman was at once all

sympathy, leaping to her side and guiding her toward one of the chairs near the window.

'Sit,' he said, and to the uniformed Lopez, 'Bring her some water, quickly.'

He held the glass for her while she took a long drink. He did not seem threatening now, but rather kind and gentle. Still, even in her dazed state, she could not help seeing the significance of his visit here.

'You said — ' She stumbled over the word. ' — murdered. But surely that can't be . . . '

Mendoza shook his head sadly. 'Alas, it is so. She was found in her bed this morning, apparently dead for some hours. Tests were made. There was poison in the tea she drank before going to bed — you knew that she always had a pot of tea before retiring?'

'Yes, I lived at the palace for some time. I knew it was her regular routine,' she said, before she realized that she might be incriminating herself. 'But I hope you don't think I had anything to do with this.'

'No, of course not,' he said, but altogether too glibly to be convincing. 'But the facts, you see, suggest someone who was familiar with the house and with the Senhora's daily routine. Someone who would have known, for instance, that it was the Senhora's habit to have tea at bedtime, and that it was brought up while she was in her bath. Someone who would have known of a box of poison for rodents, in a kitchen closet. But there is another problem. Miss Amelie, the housekeeper, made the tea in the kitchen and drank a little of it herself, with no ill effect, before taking it upstairs to leave in her mistress's room. Which means, you see, that someone came into the bedroom and poisoned the tea after the housekeeper had gone back out.'

'But if someone had come into the house, surely the servants would have known,' Elizabeth said.

'I am told that by this time of evening the servants are usually in a basement room, in front of the television. If someone had rung the bell, of course . . . but no one did. So we are left with

189

only a few possibilities. Perhaps someone in the house did this, but the sister, Maria, was out at the theater. She was seen there. And Senhor Drayton is away. We have already been in touch with authorities in Rio. He has been there. There were only servants in the house, who would seem to have no reason.'

'Mrs. Drayton was a difficult task-mistress.'

He shrugged. 'I have no doubt. Still, that seems little enough motive for murdering someone, don't you think?'

'And you think I have a reason?' Elizabeth lifted an eyebrow. 'Yes, I can see how it must look to you. But of course I was not in the house.'

'Of course. Still, unless someone broke in — and there is no sign of this — the person we are seeking must have been someone with a key. Have you a key to the Bishop's Palace, Senhorita?'

Elizabeth's throat felt so dry she could barely speak. 'Yes, I have one. But there must be others.'

'Yes, surely,' Senhor Mendoza agreed quickly, smoothly. 'Senhor Drayton has one, of course. We will see when he returns if he has it with him. And the Senhora had one herself; it is with her things. Perhaps you know of some other key?'

She stared into the dark, watchful eyes and shook her head slowly. So far as she knew, there were no other keys. She knew that Maria did not have one. She could see in the Brazilian's eyes how things looked to him. She had a key. She had a motive. She'd had the opportunity.

'Perhaps if you could tell me how you spent your evening,' he suggested, his tone of voice never varying from its ingratiating softness. 'After, say, nine o'clock.'

'I came to my room after dinner and went to bed about that time. I haven't been out since.'

'And there is someone, perhaps, who could substantiate this?' he asked, and at the flick of anger across her face, added quickly, 'Perhaps a maid came in during the night on an errand, or you got a telephone call through the hotel's switchboard? Anything of this nature would be helpful.'

'No, nothing,' she said. 'I saw no one

and talked to no one.'

'That is most unfortunate.' He walked to the window and gazed thoughtfully from it for a moment.

'Am I under arrest?' she asked bluntly.

He paused for a second or two before he answered. 'But indeed, no. At the present we are only investigating. However, if you would be so kind as to remain in Manalos until our investigations are completed, we would be grateful.'

As they were preparing to leave, Senhor Mendoza paused to ask one final question. 'There is one thing,' he said. 'Perhaps you will know why Senhor Drayton returned so soon to Rio.'

'Yes. He was trying to raise money to buy the Drayton line from his wife.'

'Ah. But that will not be necessary now, though.' He nodded his head and went out.

* * *

Karl was back first thing in the morning, looking haggard from his hectic trip and the news of Kitty's death. He came directly to the hotel but he had been in Elizabeth's room no more than a minute when someone knocked at the door. Elizabeth opened it to find Senhor Mendoza there.

'I thought we might talk with Senhor Drayton,' he said, smiling. It was an effective reminder to Elizabeth that the police were keeping a very close eye on her.

Karl went with them and returned shortly. It was a strange reunion for the lovers. There was no sense of freedom. The woman who had stood in their way was dead, but in another sense she was even more decidedly between them now than she had been before. They could not ignore the very real possibility that Elizabeth might be arrested and charged with murder.

'Looking at things from their point of view,' she said, 'I'm surprised they haven't already done so.'

'They are exercising all due caution,' he said. 'If they were wrong, they would be offending me, and I will inherit most of the Deodora wealth. So they are thinking to the future. They will want to be very sure.'

'If only there were some clue pointing to someone else,' she said. 'But unless we suspect one of the servants or a burglar, no one else had access to the house at the right time. And would this burglar have known Kitty's routine? Whoever did this had to know that she was accustomed to soaking in a tub while her tea was brought in and left in her room.'

'An intruder could have been acting on someone else's behalf. Even on mine, if you think of it. I might have wanted Kitty dead. It would not be difficult in Manalos to find someone who could arrange that, for the right price. I would only have to leave my key with him.'

'But you had your key with you,' Elizabeth said. 'Didn't you?'

'You see, even you cannot deny it is a possibility.'

'But why would you want to murder Kitty? She had agreed to give you a divorce; she was even agreeable to your buying the line.'

'But you only know that because I told you it was so.'

'I know it is so because I know you,'

she said emphatically. 'You didn't kill her.'

He sighed. 'No, I didn't. And neither did you. I am only suggesting how it might have been done. And there's no shortage of people with motive. Kitty spent most of her life forcing people to do as she wanted, and she wasn't always scrupulous in her methods. There's Maria; you could hardly blame her if she wanted to see her sister dead after all these years. She's probably wished it often enough. And there's that actor, Clark Bennet. I've always thought there was something peculiar in Kitty's friendship with him.'

'Yes, I thought so too. She seemed to have some sort of hold over him. But would he kill her for it? Besides, there's a lack of opportunity again. He was acting in a play at the time. It's no use, darling. When you get right down to it, I'm the one with the perfect motive, and the means.'

He took her in his arms and kissed the tip of her nose. 'There's just one thing wrong with that theory,' he said. 'I know you didn't kill Kitty either.'

'But who did?'

12

Again and again, Elizabeth asked herself that same question over the next few days. Who had killed Kitty Drayton? How, and why? But she came no closer to an answer.

The funeral was held three days later. It was a Sunday and the people of Manalos turned out in droves — as much, Elizabeth suspected, to see her and Karl as to pay their respects to Kitty.

She could not look around without seeing dozens of pairs of eyes upon her. She felt sure most of them, in their minds, had already seen her convicted and hung. She could hardly blame them.

She did not know if the police had come up with any new information. They had apparently decided she was not going to try to flee the city and they had ceased watching her so closely, but that may have been nothing more than confidence in the fact that Manalos was not an easy city to flee. She had no doubt the airport was watched — easy enough, since there was only one flight in and out each day. And if she left by boat — Karl's, perforce — they could easily overtake her. Only someone really desperate would attempt the journey through the jungle, with half the width of a continent to cross.

She became belatedly aware that the minister was giving Kitty's eulogy. She thought of the poor creature being laid to rest. How she had connived and plotted to dominate the lives of others, and in the end her own life had been wrested from her. Not in the natural course of things, either, but to some evil end.

Her eyes went around the crowd of mourners. Probably someone here was the guilty one. If only she could look into their hearts, what would she find? Did any one of them truly grieve, despite their show of mourning? It was told around town that Maria had taken to bed the moment she had learned the news of her sister's death, and even here throughout the funeral service she was being held up by Amelie the housekeeper on one side and Clark Bennet on the other.

Potter stood nearby with little Caroline, who looked more honestly bored than any of the adults. According to Karl, Potter and Caroline were moving out of the palace today. Most of the servants would in fact be leaving. They had worked for the Deodoras, but now Karl was master of the palace, and many of them had not chosen to stay and serve a new master.

At Elizabeth's insistence, Karl had taken his place at the front as chief mourner. But when the services ended he came to where she was standing, ignoring the glances of the mourners drifting out of the churchyard.

'Where are we going?' she asked as they walked together.

'To the palace.'

She glanced sideways at him. 'Do you think that's wise?'

'Entirely wise. I have to go through Kitty's personal things and I want you to help. Maybe we can find some clue there.'

★   ★   ★

The trouble was, though, that neither of them was trained as an investigator, and neither had any idea what they might be looking for.

'Anything that would seem to imply a motive would be helpful,' he said, going through a folder filled with correspondence. He took out a letter and read through it hurriedly. 'Like this, for example,' he said. 'It's from Kitty's attorneys. Apparently it's a cover letter that accompanied a new will.'

'That might be interesting.'

'It says that the will has been changed in accordance with her instructions and that the draft of the new will is enclosed for her approval. Listen to this — the bequest previously left to Mr. Clark Bennet has been deleted, per her instructions.'

He paused and exchanged glances with Elizabeth. 'The rest remains the same. Maria is to receive a trust fund from which she will be paid an allowance, and the bulk of the estate comes to me.' He looked up. 'I suspect if she'd lived a few days longer, there'd have been some more changes made.'

'I wonder if she actually went through with these.'

'Probably. The lawyers have the final will. It's to be read the day after tomorrow. But she wouldn't have had time to disinherit me between the time we had our discussion and the time she died.'

'Clark will be disappointed. I'm sure he expected to be named.'

'I'm surprised by that too. Apparently he was named at one time. Why do you suppose she changed her mind? And did he know? She went right on being as friendly with him as before.'

Elizabeth had been riffling through some paid receipts. 'She certainly took an active interest in his career. There's an entire collection of his notices in here with the receipts. And her contributions to the theater went up sharply after he joined the company.'

Karl was thoughtful for a moment. 'We've been thinking of receiving money as a motive for murder, but suppose Kitty was killed because someone wasn't receiving any? Suppose Clark found out he'd been disinherited and killed her in anger?'

'When was that letter written?'

He glanced at it again. 'Three months ago.'

'So he could hardly have been acting on impulse. And you know Clark; he's a conniver with a very high opinion of himself. If he'd known she'd disinherited him, he'd have been more likely to want to keep her alive, wouldn't he, and try to change her mind again?'

'Maybe. What about Maria?'

'According to that letter, she fares about the same either way, I'd say. A small allowance. What's this?'

She had been removing a carton from the bottom of Kitty's closet. As she pulled it forward, a newspaper-wrapped bundle leaning against the wall fell forward.

'Looks like pictures.' Karl took the bundle out of the closet and laid it flat on the bedroom floor. 'Something in frames, anyway. Probably more of the Deodora ancestors.'

'Not stuck away in a closet. Not the way she liked to brag about them.'

201

He struggled with the twine and finally went to Kitty's dressing table for a pair of cuticle scissors to cut it. When he tore back the brown wrapping paper they found three framed portraits, two of them photographs and the other done in colored chalk, common to the sidewalk artists in Rio. The pictures were all of the same handsome man with long black hair and a thick moustache.

'Who do you suppose he is?' Elizabeth asked.

'Here's something. A passport. It was wrapped with the portraits.'

He flicked the passport open. The same man looked somberly back at them. 'Walter Prescott,' he read the name on the passport. 'Kitty's first husband. So that's the man I was forever being compared to. I always came out second best, you know. I never could figure out why, if he was so wonderful, she settled for me anyway.'

He tossed the passport aside. Elizabeth was studying one of the photographs intently, holding it so the light from the window fell on it.

'Darling, maybe it's only my imagination, but doesn't Mr. Prescott look like someone we know?' she asked.

He came to look over her shoulder. 'Bennet, you mean? You may be right. There's certainly more than a passing resemblance.'

'That could mean something,' Elizabeth said excitedly. 'Walter was older than Kitty, wasn't he? He might have been Clark's father, mightn't he?'

'Yes, maybe one of those under-the-stairways romances with a housemaid. That would explain Kitty's great interest in him. But not her suddenly disinheriting him. And it still doesn't give him a motive for murder.'

Elizabeth rubbed one of her temples with the tips of her fingers. 'I still can't help thinking that Clark figures in this somehow.' She remembered that night in Rio and the Death figure pursuing her. It could have been Clark, regardless of what he and Kitty had said afterward. And he might not have been only trying to frighten her. Was he capable of murder? On the surface he was harmless, but a man that vain, that self-centered . . . If he thought his interests were being crossed . . . It was hard to say.

Something popped into her mind, something she had forgotten until this moment. 'Wait . . . Clark might have had a key,' she said. 'I just remembered. It was Clark who took Kitty's key to have a duplicate made for me. He could have had two copies made then.'

Karl's expression mirrored her excitement. 'That shouldn't be too hard to check,' he said. 'There aren't that many key shops in town that could duplicate an old-fashioned key like that one. And there's one right near the theater. I've never used it, but I remember seeing it, on a little back street near the stage door. That would be the logical place for him to have a copy made.'

'Or copies. Do you think we should pass this information on to the police?'

He helped her to her feet. 'We can start by checking it out ourselves. If we find that Mr. Bennet did have an extra key made, we'll have something concrete to take to Senhor Mendoza, something he can't just ignore.'

'You don't think he's very interested in clues at this point, do you?'

'I think just now he feels sure you're his girl, and he's just waiting for you to do something rash, like trying to slip out of the city. The system here is sometimes a little lax.'

The house was quiet as they let themselves out. Maria had reportedly gone back to bed when she returned from the funeral and the servants were nowhere to be seen. They walked together toward the neighborhood of the theater.

'It's Sunday,' she said aloud. 'Maybe the key shop won't be open.'

'Can't tell till we get there. These little shops don't always follow a regular opening and closing schedule, I'm afraid. But it won't be a wasted trip anyway. I want you to tackle Senhora Costa.'

'The theater manageress? But why?'

'Just generally to see what you can find out about Kitty and Clark. It's the sort of thing a woman could pry out of another woman more easily than a man could. Besides, she's never much cared for me.'

'I don't imagine she'll care for me if I start interrogating her.'

'You don't need to say you're looking for clues to Kitty's murder, of which she most likely already considers you guilty. And you needn't mention that you've been going through Kitty's private papers. Just tell her you understand my wife was a patron and you think you might be coming into a little money and you'd like to know a bit about the local theater. Let her think you're a woman who's about to come across with something. And while you're at it, see what she tells you about Clark Bennet and his relationship with Kitty.'

'If she tries to explain the business end of the theater, I won't have any idea what she's talking about.'

'She won't want you to. Keep saying, 'Oh,' and 'You don't say,' and then bring the conversation around to the actors. She'll tell you everything. The theater is usually desperate for nice, guileless patrons.'

They had arrived at the key shop. It was something of a jumble, with every conceivable sort of metal and wire on shelves on the floor, and on the filthy little counter that stretched the shop's width, all of it generously festooned with cobwebs.

They waited for a few minutes and when no one came, Karl banged on the counter with his hand and shouted toward the door at the rear. At last an old man, stooped and withered like a raisin, came in. They soon discovered that he was nearly stone-deaf and he spoke only a very crude English. Karl tackled him in Portuguese, with no greater success.

'It's some sort of dialect,' Karl said in frustration.

At last the man's wife appeared to interpret. By now the locksmith was studying the key Elizabeth had produced. It was, he told them through his wife, an old pattern, of which very few were in use any longer, even here in Manalos. Most people today had the Yale-type lock with its smaller and much-handier-to-carry key. And the Yale lock was safer, too: those old-fashioned locks were notoriously easy to pick, and simply no deterrent to a determined burglar.

He had a splendid flow of such information, which it took doubly long to deliver since it first had to be told in dialect to his wife and then translated for them. His deafness made it difficult and counter-productive to interrupt him and they could only wait impatiently, trusting that in time he would come back to the subject of Elizabeth's key, now resting on the counter between them. If this man had made a copy, it must have been this exact key from which he had worked, and Elizabeth hoped that the sight of it might recall the circumstances to him.

At last the wife said that, yes, her husband had worked from that very key some weeks before. A young man from the theater had brought it in to be copied.

'You're sure it's the same key?' Karl asked.

The woman translated his question, listened to her husband's lengthy reply, and said, 'Yes, he is certain. He had to keep the young man waiting because at the time he had only one suitable blank in stock, and the gentleman wanted two copies, so he had to return a bit later that same day.'

'Then he made two copies?' Karl asked.

The old man looked startled by the excitement in Karl's voice, but he understood the question all right, and nodded his head vigorously. 'Si, senhor,' he said. 'Two.'

Karl made some vague remarks about a key he wanted copied but didn't happen to have with him at the moment and pressed some money into the old man's hand. In a moment he and Elizabeth were outside the shop, beaming with excitement.

'So Clark did have a key,' she said. 'And a motive if he still believed he was getting an inheritance. And of course he has an alibi, but with all the time in the world to plan things, he would have, wouldn't he? Clark Bennet is our murderer, I'm sure of it . . . '

She paused when Karl gave her arm a fierce squeeze. She looked around and found herself staring straight into Clark Bennet's eyes.

13

'I was just on my way to the theater,'
Clark said, stopping to chat.

The three of them were so over-
whelmingly polite and happy to see one
another that Elizabeth thought anyone
must see the enthusiasm was bogus.
She left the conversation to Karl and
contented herself with gaping pleasantly
and hoping she had not been speaking
loudly enough for Clark to have heard.
He didn't show that he had, but then he
was an actor.

The conversation was fortunately brief.
They parted with comments of regret at
having seen so little of one another recently
and mutual promises to amend that situation. When he had gone, Elizabeth felt as
if she had been holding her breath the
entire time.

'Do you think he heard me?' she asked.

Karl shook his head. 'Impossible to tell.
I don't think so.' He glanced at his watch.

'There's just time for you to tackle Senhora Costa.'

'Oh, darling, couldn't you come, too? I'm no good at this detective business, honestly, and my nerves are frayed enough from bumping into Clark.'

'No, you go, my dear. We might have a very nice social visit if I came and we'd certainly provide her with some dirt for her lady friends, but I doubt that we'd get any real information. No, if she's going to tell us anything, it's going to be in the form of good old-fashioned gossip, and that, I'm afraid, is more down your alley than mine.'

'Sometime later I'll quarrel with you over that, but I suppose on the face of it, you're right. Where shall I meet you?'

'There's a little cafe just around that corner there,' he said, pointing. 'The prices are high, the food is tasteless and unvaried and the service is virtually nonexistent.'

'Good heavens, why go at all? Why not pick someplace better?' she asked with a laugh.

'Because that particular cafe is fre- quented by the actors from the theater, who sometimes come in during the show, even in their makeup, for a quick cup of coffee. I may be able to pick up some information as well.'

They parted, he to the cafe and she to the theater, where she found Senhora Costa thrilled to see her. The theater manageress was a frail little woman who wore an air of desperate graciousness superimposed over frantic uncertainty. She expressed her regret at the unfortunate happenings at the palace.

'I know how awkward it must be for you,' she said. 'And of course Senhorita Deodora must be very lonely without her sister and lifelong companion.'

'I'm sure she is,' Elizabeth murmured. Personally she thought Maria was probably happy to be free of Kitty's domination.

'She was here the night of her sister's death,' Senhora Costa said. 'I recall we spoke in the lounge before the play began. She asked if I thought she would enjoy it, and I hardly knew what to tell her. It was a local thing, you know, by a local playwright, and about local history, and it was a little clumsy in spots. But local people do come, you understand, and they like to hear the references to their ancestors, and the box office did very well for the week. Anyway, I needn't have worried. The senhorita saw me on her way out and told me she had enjoyed it very much. She's always been so nice to us. An agreeable person, but overshadowed by her sister. Senhora Kitty's personality was so very strong. We shall all miss her.'

She seemed to add a question mark at the end of the last remark, perhaps wondering if the two of them might not somehow ensure that the senhora's personality would not be too sadly missed in the little theater.

Elizabeth took her cue from this and mentioned Kitty's shares in the theater, with the explanation that Mr. Drayton had felt he knew too little about the theater and so had asked her to look into the matter for him. She thought it gave her the perfect justification for her inquiries.

For a while, though, they were at cross

purposes. Senhora Costa feared that Elizabeth expected some sort of dividend on the shares and Elizabeth had to reassure her that, in her view, supporting such a theater was more in the line of an obligation to the general public than a matter of vulgar profit. They were instantly at one and Senhora Costa warmed visibly toward her guest.

'The Deodoras have always supported our little venture,' she said. 'And Senhora Kitty's first husband, Mr. Prescott, was an amateur writer, one of whose plays we produced on our very stage — at something of a loss, unfortunately, but Senhora Kitty made up the difference personally.'

Elizabeth worked the conversation around to Clark. Senhora Costa seemed to retreat a little from this subject. She was enthusiastic about his work, but offered very little beyond that. Elizabeth could see from the slightly raised eyebrows that the Senhora was wondering just what her interest could be in this young man. No doubt, Elizabeth thought, this too would be discussed at some length with her woman friends later.

Well, she hadn't come here to try to save her already tarnished reputation. She plunged determinedly forward.

'Mr. Bennet is really good, then?' she asked.

'Oh, yes, and well liked, which is important in a little group like ours. For our company to work, it's essential that everyone get along together.'

'I'm not quite clear — what is his connection with the Deodoras?' Elizabeth asked, trying without complete success to sound guileless.

Senhora Costa visibly withdrew still further. 'I don't know that there is what could be called a connection, properly speaking,' she said. 'Senhora Kitty had an interest in the young man, but only in his career, I am sure. It is my understanding, in fact, that they did not even meet personally until she sent him a request after one of his performances. It was, he liked to say, sort of a royal command. She could be a little theatrical in her gestures. No one took offense, you understand.' She smiled faintly, as if to say she did not mean to reveal any more.

'Of course I may have gotten a false impression about her interest in Mr. Bennet,' Elizabeth said. 'Since Mr. Drayton has implied that he will want my advice, I naturally wanted to continue to sponsor anyone with whom she was particularly concerned. She left only the vaguest indications and I thought it my duty to see if there were anything there of significance. But as there is not . . . '

The words came now in a rush. 'As a matter of fact, the first I learned of her very great interest in Mr. Bennet was when I received a note along with her annual check — just one of those brief, unsigned notes she sometimes sent around, such as when she wanted a different seat or had especially enjoyed a play. You do understand, she was one of our chief patrons, and we always paid attention to any opinions she offered.'

'Of course. And she suggested you engage Mr. Bennet?'

'Yes. She gave us the name of the agency he was with. He was in Rio, you see, but between roles. We wrote the agency, which sent us his portfolio, and as he seemed quite suitable we asked him to come for a try-out. He was very good, and we gave him a contract — which, I might say, we have never regretted.'

Elizabeth had her own opinions of Clark Bennet's talents, but she kept them to herself and asked instead, 'Still, you don't think they knew one another?'

'Oh, no, I'm sure they did not. I had an impression she was obliging an old friend. Nearly everyone has some friend or acquaintance whose cousin or nephew or what-have-you wants to go on the stage. We are quite accustomed to such requests, although they do not usually bring us anyone so satisfactory as Mr. Bennet.'

Nor as well sponsored, Elizabeth thought. 'Did Mr. Bennet know how he came to be hired?' she asked.

Her question seemed to rub the wrong way. Senhora Costa's tone was a little cooler when she said, 'Well, he was hired because of his talent. But as to who suggested him to us, no, he did not know, I'm sure. Senhora Kitty's note said specifically she did not want him to be told, and in fact she proved rather — oh, what shall I say? — touchy about it.'

'Oh? In what way?'

'Nothing much came up about all this until a few months ago, when I had occasion to write to her on some other matter, and I told her how pleased I was with her protégé. The next day she arrived looking quite put out, and demanded to know why I referred to him in that way.

'Of course I produced her note and she even admitted, a bit reluctantly, that the wording could lead one to think of him that way, though that was not what had been intended. It was all most unpleasant. I had the feeling I had made some mistake, without quite knowing what. She said very little, mind you, but she had the most awful look on her face for a while. She went away and for several weeks she did not attend the theater at all. I was frightened that I had offended her. Then, just like that, she started coming again, as regularly as before. Whatever the problem had been, it had all blown over.'

Someone of the theater staff had twice come to the door of the senhora's office, obviously hoping to catch her free. Elizabeth thought she had learned as much as she was likely to, and she rose to go.

'Of course I have no real authority in the matter,' she said, 'but I shall certainly recommend to Mr. Drayton that he continue his wife's support of your theater.' She meant to do just that, too. It would be wrong, she felt, to raise the hopes of this harassed creature without making due payment.

She was almost to the theater's exit when someone caught her by the arm and she turned to discover it was Clark. He had been standing behind a piece of scenery, smoking a cigarette, and she got the impression he had been waiting for her. It unnerved her a little. She wondered if he might have been near enough to Senhora Costa's office to have listened to their conversation. She tried to visualize the scene. Most of the time the door had been closed. Would their voices have carried through the thin walls?

'Hello,' Clark said, smiling brightly. 'Going to meet your friend?'

'Mr. Drayton? No, he had business to attend to,' she said. 'He went his own way earlier.'

'In that case, as long as you're on your own, come and talk to me while I put on my makeup.'

She tried not to look too unhappy at that suggestion. There were few prospects she could think of just at the moment less attractive to her than spending time alone with Clark in his dressing room. 'Isn't that against the rules?' she asked.

'Well, it's Sunday, and it's only a matinee. I don't suppose they'll put us before a firing squad. Come along, I could use the company. That's a girl.'

She came, feeling just as she would if she'd been asked to put her head in a lion's mouth. She thought of Karl waiting in the little cafe around the corner. By now he must surely be getting impatient. Maybe he would come looking for her.

Clark ushered her into his dressing room, sat her on a small cane-seated chair and took off his jacket. He wrapped himself in a robe and began to rub makeup over his mobile features.

'It's been ages since we've seen one another,' he said. He put rust and ochre greasepaint on his face in rather garish-looking stripes, making her wonder what role he was making up for.

'No more than an hour,' she said.

He laughed and said, 'Well, yes, that's so, if you count accidentally bumping into one another on the street.'

It was true that, even before Kitty's death and the trip to Rio, she had mostly avoided Clark. To be seen with someone like Clark was to court a publicity she hadn't wanted, nor did she want to encourage him to think there might be some romance in store for them.

Anyway, he could be exhausting. He was the sort who always had to be played up to. His compliments could sparkle and flash but after a time his interest in anyone other than himself flagged. Kitty had suggested often that Clark was smitten by Elizabeth, but she herself felt that no woman would ever turn the needle of his compass from its unvarying attraction — himself.

But she did not want to antagonize him

just at the moment. 'I've been busy,' she said lamely.

'That's never prevented anyone from doing what he wanted to do,' he said good-naturedly.

'Well, for that matter, you could have come to see me.' She tried to make that sound mildly coquettish.

'Without an invitation?'

'That never stopped you before.'

He laughed and said, 'Well, I did have a standing invitation to the palace, but not from you, and certainly not from the grim Mr. Drayton.' He began putting shadows around his eyes. 'Besides, I've always thought the boys hung around you like flies.'

'For the most part the boys I like have managed to stay away. At least until recently.' She had been thinking of Karl, but from the way Clark perked up and smoothed his shiny hair, she realized he thought she had meant him. What a monumental ego the man had!

He gave her a glance in the mirror, through lowered lashes, as he put powder over the paint on his face and went behind a screen to change into his stage clothes. When he came out he smoothed his hair again and took up a hand mirror to inspect the sides and back.

Satisfied at last, he put the mirror atop the dressing table and turned to her. She found herself staring at him with a strange sort of fascination. The corners of his eyes were red and his eyelids outlined in dark blue. His hair gleamed darkly, his face was garishly bright, his lips carmine. He was like some otherworldly creature, beautiful in a grotesque manner, and unnerving in the way he stared at her, his gaze not wavering.

'Do I look all right?' he asked after a very long silence.

'Quite the lady killer,' she said inanely, nervous, and when she realized what she had said she felt a prickling on her scalp and knew she was turning crimson.

He did not seem taken aback by that stupid remark, however. 'I suppose it's a little ridiculous to watch a man paint his face like this and posture before a mirror,' he said. 'It's only a part of acting, a little part, but it has to be done. Besides, here in Manalos, I only get to kill older ladies. The young prefer Brad Pitt and Tom Cruise, just as they do elsewhere.'

Kill older ladies . . . the words seemed to reverberate in her mind. Could he really have said that, if it were true? Or was his poise so perfect, his acting ability sufficient for that test?

Noises from outside had begun to intrude on their conversation. Someone was tapping on doors saying, 'Overtures and beginners, please.'

She was grateful when the knock came at Clark's door. 'I suppose I'd better go,' she said.

'There's no hurry. I'm not on for several minutes yet. Now, if this were last week we could have practically the whole second act together. Plenty of time for me to show you what an enjoyable companion I can be.'

She started to get up from her chair but he motioned her back into it. She sat, hoping he could not see how badly her hands were shaking.

'How'd you like my little friend, the key-maker?' he asked. 'Rather like the

Sorcerer's Apprentice, isn't he? He could only exist in Manalos, or maybe in a bad ballet. If you put him on stage in a play they'd say he was overdone. Were you able to get any sense out of him? It's a bit of a challenge.'

She thought her voice sound strained when she said, 'Oh, yes, he'll be able to do what Mr. Drayton wants.'

'Quite a joke I had, when I took Kitty's key to be copied,' he said in a studiedly casual tone. 'Did I ever tell you about that?'

No, oh no, Clark, you never told me, she thought. *You never mentioned it. Odd that you should feel the need to do so now, when you've just seen me coming out of that shop. But go on, Clark, do tell me. And, Lord, don't let me bat an eye, no matter how far-fetched his explanation might be, because I don't want to be done silently to death in this dingy dressing room — strangled, maybe — and not found for forty years until someone in the distant future stumbles over a newly discovered skeleton...*

14

Clark licked his forefinger and cleaned off a speck of powder that had clung to an eyelash.

'Well,' he said, 'I'd been over to tea with her majesty, you remember, and she asked me to have an extra key made for you. But when I left and got outside, I heard the patter of little feet behind me and there was Maria, all out of breath, running down the street after me. She asked me if I would have two keys made instead of one. It seems, so she told me, that Kitty had never considered Maria responsible enough to have a key of her own. Would you believe that?'

'I'd believe anything,' she said, with all the conviction she could muster.

'Of course, she didn't say anything against Dame Kitty — she never did — but one could see it weighed heavily on her mind. You know, sometimes the little things do that more than the big ones. They say it's the trivialities that one murders for, not the big fortunes and the great loves, the way the novelists have it.'

He paused and looked speculatively at her, and not for anything in the world would she have been able to make a reply to that statement. She sat mutely, her lips slightly parted, and stared at him with rapt attention.

'Anyway, to shorten the story,' he went on, 'when I got to the shop, I had two keys cut. I suppose the old man told you that?'

You must lie to him, a voice in her head said. *Tell him you know nothing about that*. She nodded silently.

'I supposed as much. Anyway, the next time I came around, I slipped it into Maria's hand under the tea table. I felt like I was playing a scene out of *Conspiracy in the Dormitory*, or *The Worst Girl at St. Albertine's*. Poor old thing. It must have been grim for her to live under her sister's thumb like that.'

For a moment, he had convinced her. In the first place, she wanted desperately to be convinced; but more than that, it was a good story, founded on probability, and she could hardly think he had just made this up on the spur of the moment.

But then, it wasn't the spur of the moment at all. He'd had all that time since he'd seen them coming out of the key shop. He would know what they would learn there, and he'd had plenty of time to get his story straight. Time, even, since he was an actor, to rehearse it so that he could make it sound utterly convincing.

She got to her feet, conscious of that queer strangling sensation one gets in one's throat when something very dramatic is about to happen in a play. Only, she did not want anything dramatic to happen just now.

'I must go,' she said. 'Thank you for letting me come in and see the wheels go around, so to speak. I've enjoyed it.'

She had taken no more than a step before he had moved in front of her, between her and the door. 'Wait,' he said. He took hold of her shoulders. 'Aren't you going to kiss me for good luck?'

She could not answer him. Her smile

was actually painful to maintain, and she could only stare into his eyes the way a mongoose must watch the cobra who is about to strike. She knew she could not possibly endure his kiss without screaming her bloody head off, and she couldn't think how she could possibly avoid it.

Luckily, that problem was solved for her. The door opened suddenly and an owlish-looking young man said peevishly, 'Don't you know you're on in about one minute?'

'Lord, yes, I hadn't realized it was so late,' Clark said, and let Elizabeth go. She practically ran down the young man in the doorway getting through it.

'No need to see me out,' she called over her shoulder. 'I know the way.'

She looked back once to see him half-running toward the stage. She fled out the exit door and hurried on unsteady legs to the cafe where Karl waited, but before she had quite gotten there she met him in the street, strolling in her direction.

'I was coming to look for you,' he said. 'I was beginning to think that woman had hit you on the head and stuffed you into a trunk.'

'No, she was very helpful, in fact. To tell you the truth, I've been with Clark in his dressing room.'

He looked appropriately surprised by her news. 'I think you'd better let me buy you a drink while you tell me about it,' he said, piloting her back to the cafe.

He ordered them rum punches and waited until they had been served. Then he leaned toward her across the postage-stamp-sized table. 'So, I suppose you just popped in to warn him that we were planning on blaming him for the murder. I guess I ought to have suspected something of the sort.'

'It was nothing at all like that. He caught me leaving the theater and practically dragged me into his dressing room. Anyway, I thought I might learn something if I went.'

'And did you?'

'Yes, plenty.' She began with her interview with Senhora Costa and related her experience through the meeting with Clark. 'According to him, he got the extra key made for Maria, because she asked him for one and he saw it as a subtle form of rebellion on her part. It could almost be true, couldn't it? I do know Maria didn't have her own key.'

'Yes, it could almost be true. I know Kitty was difficult with Maria. But I've learned a few things too. For one thing, in that play last week, *The Cradle of the King*, Clark had an offstage wait of three quarters of an hour — part of the first act and almost all of the second. I've got a program right in my pocket. On two nights during the week he came here during his wait to have coffee and study his next week's part. But he did not come in on that night.'

'Then he could have gone to the house, let himself in with that door key, and gotten back to the theater in time to be in the second act.'

'Yes, it looks as if he could have done just that. If only one of the servants had seen or heard something. But Mendoza has probably checked all that out thoroughly.'

'We could talk to them ourselves.'

He made a face. 'That probably wouldn't do much good. Most of them were entirely partial to Kitty. I doubt that they'd be willing to talk frankly with either of us.'

'One of them might,' she said thoughtfully. 'There is one girl — Valerie, Amelie's niece. I sort of took her part one day when Kitty tore into her over something. She might speak freely. And if any of the others had heard or seen anything they hadn't reported to the police, she probably has heard about it.'

'Valerie Allende,' he said, looking cheered. 'Yes, I know her. Well, it's certainly worth a try anyway. Come on, I know where her mother lives, too. It's near the river. One of Valerie's brothers works for the Drayton line.'

★ ★ ★

When they arrived at the Allende cottage, however, Valerie was out. Her mother was nervous and excited to have company, especially such important company.

'And wouldn't this just be the day,' she

232

said, 'that Valerie would take it in her head to go wandering along the river. But if you would make yourselves comfortable here in the sitting room, I'll send one of the younger children for her. It won't take more than a few minutes.'

'We don't mind waiting,' Karl insisted.

After she had sent one of the small children for Valerie, Senhora Allende put herself to making her guests comfortable. She brought them glasses of a sweet fruit wine and they settled in her parlor.

'The senhora worked at the palace some years ago,' Karl said, sipping his wine. 'That was before my time there, of course. You must have known Mr. Prescott.'

'Yes, indeed.'

But if Clark was Walter's child by one of the servant girls, the Senhora either did not know or was keeping that information to herself. Her answers to Karl's gentle questioning were entirely noncommittal on that subject.

Elizabeth tried her hand, too. 'I suppose it was a more pleasant place to work in the old days,' she said, 'when things were booming.'

'Ah, well, senhorita, it was different then,' Senhora Allende said in the tone of one who has begun to reminisce. 'I was only a young girl, mind you, but I was there in the days of the Deodoras, when the senhor was alive and the senhoritas, Kitty and Maria, were young the same as me. The mother and father were lovely people, too. And Senhorita Maria, what a lovely child she was.'

'She was your favorite then?' Elizabeth asked, surprised that anyone should favor the pallid Maria over the lively Kitty.

'Oh, she was everyone's favorite. Especially her father's.'

'But he left everything to Kitty,' Elizabeth said.

The senhora nodded. 'Yes. The mother was dead by then, and Senhorita Kitty was already getting grand, and a bit imperious. But you must understand, Senhorita Kitty was not so pretty when she was young, and Maria was ravishing. I think perhaps the father thought it would make things even, to give Kitty the money. And Senhorita Maria had no sense with money. She was like a little fairytale princess, all charm and prettiness, and not a bit of common sense. If she'd had the money it would all be gone by now.'

'So their father left the money to Kitty instead,' Karl quietly encouraged her to continue.

'Yes. Oh, if he had not died so suddenly from a fall, Senhorita Maria might have wheedled it out of him. She could coax anything out of anybody. Cunning as a monkey, she was; would tell you anything and make you believe it. But she had such charm and such high spirits you didn't mind being fooled. And when you discovered the truth, why she would laugh so hard that you couldn't help laughing with her.'

She paused and in the silence Elizabeth saw the astonishment on Karl's face, and knew hers must show the same. This was a side of Maria neither of them would ever have guessed. 'Were you there,' she asked, 'in the house, after Senhorita Kitty married Mr. Prescott?'

'Well, I was there for the wedding. You

should have seen my Maria then — she was six times as lovely as the bride, and behaving wickedly, the little puss, making herself the center of attention even though it was her sister's day. But the marriage was done anyway, and Senhora Kitty went on her honeymoon with her new husband and Maria stayed home, of course. It was just a few months after they returned from the honeymoon that Senhora Kitty dismissed the servants. Except for Amelie, everyone had to go. She said the senhor wanted a clean sweep. Me, I have never set foot inside the house since.'

They heard a door open and close and a moment later Valerie ran into the room, out of breath from hurrying. With her hair down and wearing a faded cotton dress, she looked like a mere child.

On a pretext of running short of time, Karl said they had to go, but he wanted to talk with Valerie, and would she be kind enough to come partway with them and talk while they went?

They had gone only a few feet from the house before Karl came to the point. 'We want to know if you saw or heard anything on the night of my wife's death,' he said.

Valerie, looking oddly frightened, asked, 'Why do you think I can help?'

'Because,' Elizabeth said, 'you were the only servant in the house who I thought might be friendly toward us.'

'Oh, I am, senhorita,' Valerie insisted. 'Only, I do not want to get into any trouble either, and if my mother found out . . . ' She stopped and clapped a hand over her mouth.

'Found out what?' Elizabeth asked. She could see that Valerie was holding something back and that she really was frightened.

'Miss Amelie knew,' Valerie said. 'And she said not to tell anyone else. My mother would be furious if she found out.'

At the point of exasperation, Elizabeth said, 'Valerie, for heaven's sake, if she found out what?'

'About Carlos,' Valerie said. 'I am not supposed to see him; she says I am too young. But we were only together for a few minutes, not more than half an hour, and we did nothing. He did not even try to kiss me.'

Karl started to say something but Elizabeth silenced him with a gesture. They had all three come to a halt in the street, and there was no one else around to overhear.

'Let me get this straight,' Elizabeth said in her most patient voice. 'You were with Carlos that night and not in the basement with the other servants, is that right?'

Valerie nodded, her eyes wide and anxious in her thin face.

'And where were the two of you?'

'In the garden. By the wall, so no one would see us.'

'Then,' Elizabeth said, hardly able to contain her excitement, 'you would have seen anyone coming or going from the house.'

'Yes, but senhorita, if there had been anything, I would have told. The policeman asked us about burglars or prowlers.'

Karl sighed and Elizabeth too could barely hide her disappointment. 'Then you saw nothing?' she asked.

'Only the senhorita herself.'

'You mean Senhora Drayton?' Karl asked.

'No, no, Senhorita Drayton.'

'Maria?' Elizabeth asked. Valerie nodded again. 'But she went to the theater that night. That would have been about eight. Do you mean you saw her leaving for the theater?'

'No, we were not in the garden that early. This was a little past nine. The senhorita came along the street very quickly — she was almost running — and she went in the front door. But she was in such a hurry she did not see us.'

'Did she ring at the front door?' Karl asked

'I do not think so. I think she had a key. Yes, I'm sure of it.'

'And that was all you saw?' Elizabeth asked.

'Yes. That, and she left again a short time later, only a minute or two, and went back the same way, again as if she were in a hurry. I just thought at the time that she had forgotten something — her gloves, perhaps — and had come home for them. But I saw no prowlers, as I told the policeman, and no strangers.'

15

'Maria,' Elizabeth said when she and Karl were alone. 'Of course.'

'Of course,' he agreed. 'No one else involved had enough anger or hatred or sheer malice in them to do it. But after all those years of suppression, all those slights, some little something happened as a match to set all that dry tinder burning.'

He rubbed the back of his neck thoughtfully. 'Senhora Allende spoke of the younger Maria as a person of natural high spirits and that she had a great deal of natural cunning, too, when it came to getting her own way. All those years under Kitty's thumb might have crushed the high spirits, but they'd only have made her more cunning. Maria lived underground, in a sense. We should have seen that, only I stayed away from the house as much as possible and you only arrived recently. All that romantic fiction she read, her pretty collections of ribbons and dried flowers, they were her life, and they had nothing to do with life as it was lived in the Bishop's Palace. She was at heart an intriguer.'

'Oh, but why murder Kitty?'

'I don't know. We'll have to ask her.'

'Ask her?'

'We have to know.'

'Do we? Couldn't we just forget all about it? It won't bring Kitty back to life. And Maria is old anyway. Maybe she didn't even know what she was doing.'

'She's not that old, and she's not crazy, either. And if we let this just fade away, both of us will live under this shadow the rest of our lives. No, my sweet, I mean to have done with all this.'

★   ★   ★

They found Maria in her sitting room at the palace. She was dressed to go out, although at the moment she was reading a romantic novel.

'I'm glad to see you've gotten up,' Elizabeth said, embarrassed by the true nature of their visit.

Maria smiled and said, 'I thought I would go out this evening, to the theater. I haven't been for some time now.'

Karl said, 'Yes, if you want to see the play they're doing this week, I think you had better go tonight. I expect by tomorrow the leading man will be gone.'

She looked alarmed. 'Clark? What do you mean? Where will he be gone?'

'Unless I'm very much mistaken, he will be under arrest by that time, for the murder of your sister.'

His words were devastating. Maria's whole body sagged in her chair and her face went an awful grayish-green color. After a moment of shock, she made an effort to straighten herself, grasping the arms of her chair to pull herself to her feet.

'Clark could not have done it,' she said. 'He was in the play that night. On stage.'

Karl shook his head. 'That alibi won't hold water. You saw that play. You know as well as I do that he was off the stage for the whole scene in the Tower of London and the scene that followed, in the forest.'

'Yes, yes, of course, but the actors never

go out, except to a little café nearby. I'm sure if you ask Clark he will account for his time.'

'I'm afraid Mr. Bennet has been unable to do so. And Mr. Bennet at least thought he had a motive. So far as he knew he was named in my wife's will. I believe he came to the house during his stage absence. He let himself in at the front door and went up to Kitty's room, where he knew her tea would be waiting for her after her bath. He dropped poison into her tea and left to return to the theater, with plenty of time to spare.'

Maria ran a tongue over her lips. 'Someone would have seen him.'

'I was away. And Elizabeth was no longer staying here. You were at the theater yourself, and the servants were all in the basement. He wasn't in much danger of running into anyone and no doubt he had some excuse ready in case he should.'

'How could he have gotten into the house without rousing the servants?' Maria demanded.

'He had a key,' Karl said. 'When he had

one made for Elizabeth, he had an extra one cut, although of course he claims he had it cut for you. But everyone knows you don't have a key. All in all, I think the locksmith's testimony will be enough to see him hanged.'

Maria lifted one hand, as if it required a great effort, and wiped her mouth. She took a deep breath. 'But if his story were true,' she said slowly, 'if he really did have that key made for me, it would change everything, wouldn't it?'

'Yes, of course. It would pretty well do away with the case against him. The key is the real proof.'

If she saw that he had set a trap for her she did not show it. She went to the dresser where her bag lay, her movements stiff and jerky, and fumbled with the clasp of her purse before she got it open. She took the house key from it and brought it to Karl. Then she sank weakly into her chair again.

Elizabeth put her hand on Karl's arm. She wished she could stop him, undo everything that had been done, but it was too late for that.

'So you had a key after all,' he said. 'And of course you were not at the play that night, or you would know there is no scene in a forest, and no scene in the Tower of London, either.'

She leaned back in the chair, listless, her eyes nearly closed. 'I don't suppose there is,' she said. 'Not that it matters very much.'

'You spoke to Senhora Costa on your way in,' Karl went on quietly, 'and again on your way out, to establish that you were there. But you left right after the curtain went up, so that you had all the time in the world to come back to the house and cold-bloodedly murder your sister. I can understand why, mind you. What I can't understand is that you were willing to fight for that actor's sake, but not for your own. Why should he matter so much to you, simply because he's Walter Prescott's son? He is Walter's son, isn't he?'

For the first time since the conversation had begun, she smiled. The pupils of her eyes widened and glowed with a sudden brilliance that transformed her face and made her look much younger. She put her head back and when she spoke it was in a tone almost of exultation.

'He's *my* son,' she said. 'Mine and Walter's.'

She looked triumphant. For a brief moment her face glowed with a terrible glory and with all the beauty that had once been hers and had faded. She was done for and she knew it, and for once in her life there was no need for secrecy and silence. Now she could boast of what she'd had to keep to herself all these years, boast of her pride and her beauty and her secret bitter revenge upon the sister who had ruled her for so long.

'It was I he loved,' she said, her voice whispering through a room that was suddenly alive with ghosts. 'All the time, he loved me. He and I met long before he even set eyes on her. One day in the square, shortly after he had come to Manalos. I was supposed to be walking with Senhora de Silva but I managed to slip away from her. I often did. I had on a yellow dress and I had gotten mud on it, and he offered me his handkerchief to clean it.

'After that we met every day, usually in

the garden down below. Of course I couldn't ask him home, because he was never formally introduced to me. Anyway, there'd have been no point. We knew he couldn't afford to marry; he hadn't any money and I hadn't any of my own either. He was frank about that. But he told me I was like wild roses to him, honeysuckle and Heart's Desire. When he talked to me like that, I didn't care about the rest of it.'

She paused for a long time. They did not try to prompt her, but waited patiently, and after a while she picked up her narrative again.

'He was introduced to Kitty at a friend's house. And Kitty was to inherit a fortune, everyone knew that — I don't know what the amount was in Brazilian currency, I've no head for figures, but it was said to be the equivalent of ten million American dollars, which even I knew was a considerable amount. He came to the house then, calling, hat in his hand, and finally he was introduced to me. I had to stand by and watch him court her, and I carried her train at the wedding, and all the time I knew that the blood in his body would never answer to any blood but mine.'

Her eyes came round to rest on Elizabeth. 'I don't suppose it ever occurred to you that ten million dollars is too much money for its possessor ever to be sure of anyone's love. In her heart, Kitty knew Walter had married her for her money. Just as you did.' She flicked a glance at Karl that made him redden, but he said nothing in reply.

'My sister was married twice, but I was loved, and that's much better. Father left the money to her because he knew she'd never disgrace him the way I would if I had it. I was extravagant and silly, and he knew Walter and I were in love — I told him so — and he knew that if the money were mine I wouldn't hesitate for a heartbeat to run off with Walter. But Father loved me. Before he died, he entrusted me to her care and made her promise she'd look after me. He thought I would be able to wheedle any material thing I really wanted out of her, the way I always had with him. But Kitty was made of sterner stuff.

'When I knew that she and Walter were to be married, I tried to go away. I begged her to give me an allowance and let me travel, but she said she had promised Father she'd look after me. It was power, power and jealousy. I knew that. She wanted me under her thumb. She couldn't bear to think I might go away and be happy. I could never have been, not without Walter, but she wouldn't let me go; she made me stay here with them and beg for every penny. For everything.

'When they came back from their honeymoon, the very first day, Walter came to me and I knew then that he loved me as much as ever. He told me he had done it because it was the only way we could be together and still have the money and the comfort he wanted for me, but that nothing could ever come between us. We were together every day after that. He made her take a rest every afternoon. She thought it was proof of his devotion to her, but that was our time to be with one another. She was a fool. And she thought she was going to have a baby. But she wasn't. I was.'

She looked at Elizabeth with unconcealed hatred. 'You laughed at me behind my back,' she said.

'No, I didn't,' Elizabeth said. 'If you want to know, I pitied you.'

Maria scoffed. 'Which is even worse. Everyone pitied me. Poor Maria, poor dim-witted spinster who had never lived life. Damn you all, I knew more of life at your age than you will ever know.'

She gave a dry bark of a laugh. 'Kitty pretended to pity me too. She, who would have given anything in the world to have what I had. After a time she realized the truth, that I was pregnant. Naturally I wouldn't tell her whose child it was. She questioned everyone and found that while she was away I had gone around wildly with numerous men, all of whom she thought undesirable. She even tried to get me married, to buy me a husband, but I refused, and finally we agreed that I'd go off with some poor little girl from the kitchen who was going to marry a planter. His name was Perreira.

'It never entered my sister's head that her own husband was my lover. People can be very near-sighted when they are in love. She even thought she was concealing the truth about my condition from him. Him, the first person I told. I was supposed to be leaving on a trip to Europe, and in the village where we went everyone thought I was some relative of the Perreiras. When the baby was born, I left him with them. They were given a generous allowance so long as I wasn't permitted any communication with the child, and he wasn't told about me, and then I was packed off for a quick trip abroad.'

16

She paused for a moment. 'In that cupboard there,' she said, pointing, 'is some sherry. I wish you'd bring me a glass.'

Karl brought it to her and she drank it down greedily, far differently from the way they'd always seen her sip her wine before.

'When I came home,' she went on, smacking her lips, 'I was virtually a prisoner. All the servants had been dismissed, and the new ones had orders to report everything I did. No more parties. No more secret meetings. I could hardly even see Walter. Then, just a short time after that, he took the fever. For three whole months he lay dying, but I never got to see him alone. Not until he was dead. They laid him out in the parlor and I slipped in there one night late, and cried over him and told him I would always love him. That was our last time together.'

She closed her eyes, but there was no sign of tears. She looked drained, and bitter.

'She mourned; she wore the widow's weeds. My heart was breaking and I couldn't even console myself with his son. She robbed me of my husband and my son and she made me sit and be humble and accept her charity every day of my life. While my son grew up never knowing me, she filled the house with pictures of the man I loved. She treated me like a child.

'I made inquiries. I learned that the plantation had failed and that the Perreiras had gone to Rio, and later that the man had died and the boy had gone on the stage. He'd changed his name and gotten some education with the money his mother got from Kitty.

'I began to think how wonderful it would be if he were here. The theater needed a leading man, and I knew that Clark must be handsome. He was Walter's son, after all. Then one day I saw an envelope on my sister's desk, addressed to the theater. It had a check in it, her usual contribution, and a little note saying she had enjoyed the most recent play. I replaced that note with another one, suggesting they hire Mr. Clark Bennet, and telling them the agency he was with. I didn't sign the note and Kitty and I wrote very much alike. It was a risk, but I thought it was worth it if they hired him, and I felt sure they would, to oblige Kitty.'

'Weren't you afraid she'd guess the truth when she saw him?' Elizabeth asked. 'You must have suspected he would look like his father.'

'Yes, I was afraid. But luck was with me; the first few times she saw him he was in character makeup. She noticed a resemblance and even commented on it, but it wasn't so noticeable as to make her suspicious, and by the time she saw him out of makeup she had gotten used to the idea of his looking like Walter. You see, it had never entered her head to distrust Walter. And when she met Clark, he gave her some story he had made up. He was ashamed of being a planter's son. You couldn't blame him for that. He must have sensed he wasn't of that class.'

'And he never knew of his connection with you?' Karl asked.

She shook her head. 'No, I was the only one who could have told him and I wouldn't do that. Everything had worked out well. Kitty took a fancy to him and I saw that would be to his advantage. I was thrilled when I learned Kitty had included him in her will. At last he was going to get what was rightfully his. He might never know the truth about me, but that wasn't important.'

Her face went ugly again. 'And then something happened to rouse Kitty's suspicions. She didn't say anything to anyone, but she came home from the theater one day in a fury and she looked through all the old records. She wouldn't speak to me at all, but she took a trip to Rio and I guessed she was going to see Senhora Perreira. I knew if she learned Clark was the child we left with them, that he was mine, she would know he must be Walter's as well.

'She came back, still without speaking to me, and she went around taking down all of Walter's portraits and putting them away. I knew then she had learned the truth. And soon after that she told me she was going to marry again.'

'So that's why she suddenly chose me the way she did,' Karl said. 'It was out of spite.'

Maria paid no attention to him. 'When Clark came here after that, Kitty was the same to him, but she began to take pleasure in humiliating me in front of him, emphasizing my dependency, sending me on errands, talking of my stupidity. She was determined to put herself before me in his eyes. It wasn't necessary. I had never dared show any affection for him. He hardly noticed me.'

She closed her eyes again with a deep sigh. 'And then I discovered that she had changed her will again, cutting him off. I knew she hadn't told him; that she was deceiving him. It was a cruel trick. She knew that in disappointing him she would be hurting me. And I decided that I wanted to kill her.'

Her eyes flew open and she gave them a bitter smile. 'And you know what is the most peculiar thing of all? I miss her. I miss her coming into the room and giving me orders. I miss all the silly habits that I laughed at her for, and her grandness and her hauteur.'

She was silent for a moment and then she stood up. She looked like a pale ghost.

'I feel now as if there is only half of me here. For the first time I am on my own and I've found that I don't like it. I'm frightened and lonely, and old. I never knew that getting used to a person matters more than being fond of her.'

She looked directly at them then, and seemed almost surprised to discover them still there.

'You needn't mourn her,' she said to Elizabeth. 'She tried to kill you. That was the whole point of taking you to Rio. It was she who persuaded Clark to try to frighten you, and the clowns to abduct you, and if you had taken the airplane back from there as she had arranged, it would have crashed in the jungle. You would never have survived the journey. But the thing is, she was determined that you should die. She'd have tried again if I hadn't killed her first. I suppose you could say I saved your life.'

She paused, as if trying to think what more she had to say. But she had said it all. 'I should like to put some things into a bag, if you don't mind. And I think I'd like a moment or so to myself.'

★ ★ ★

Karl and Elizabeth left her alone, standing desolately in the middle of her room, and went to the drawing room below. 'You're crying,' he said. 'Don't. None of this was your fault. And poor Maria . . . '

'It isn't Maria. I was thinking of poor Kitty. No one ever cared for her in her entire life, not even her beloved Walter. And now she's dead, cheated even of the memory of a faithful husband. How awful to grow old and lonely and know that you have never been loved.'

He put his arms around her. 'That's something that can never happen to you.' He lifted her face with one hand and kissed her.

It was a long time before they

remembered Maria and went to look for her. Her rooms were empty.

'I suppose we must call the police,' Elizabeth said, feeling miserable.

'Yes, we must.'

The police searched for several hours. No one thought to search the theater where the evening performance, starring Clark Bennet, had begun. When the play ended and the cleaning people came, they found her seated in the family box in her usual seat, an empty bottle in her lap that, as it turned out, had held more of the same poison that had killed Kitty. Her eyes were still open, staring at the stage where, a short time before, a dark-haired young man had acted the part of a murderer in a play.

She was still smiling when they found her.

THE END

We do hope that you have enjoyed reading this large print book.

Did you know that all of our titles are available for purchase?

We publish a wide range of high quality large print books including:
Romances, Mysteries, Classics
General Fiction
Non Fiction and Westerns

Special interest titles available in large print are:
The Little Oxford Dictionary
Music Book, Song Book
Hymn Book, Service Book

Also available from us courtesy of Oxford University Press:
Young Readers' Dictionary
(large print edition)
Young Readers' Thesaurus
(large print edition)

For further information or a free brochure, please contact us at:
Ulverscroft Large Print Books Ltd.,
The Green, Bradgate Road, Anstey,
Leicester, LE7 7FU, England.
Tel: (00 44) **0116 236 4325**
Fax: (00 44) **0116 234 0205**

Other titles in the
Linford Mystery Library:

MISTER BIG

Gerald Verner

Behind all the large-scale crimes of recent years, the police believe there is an organising genius. The name by which this mysterious personality has become familiar to the press, the police and the underworld is Mister Big. When murder and kidnapping are added to his crimes, Superintendent Budd of Scotland Yard becomes actively involved. Eventually the master detective uncovers a witness who has actually observed and recognised Mister Big leaving the scene of a murder — but before he can tell Budd whom he has seen, he is himself murdered!

FIVE GREEN MEN

V. J. Banis

Nancy's vacation at her aunt's San Francisco mansion takes a nightmarish turn when she is attacked by a mysterious thief of ancient jade figurines. Her assailant's vows to kill her are very nearly successful more than once. Can she trust the stranger who has been following her ever since her arrival in the city, even though his intervention saves her life? Then she must contend with a murder she is powerless to stop, and the return of her father, who she'd been told had died when she was a child . . .

THE SCENT OF HEATHER

V. J. Banis

Maggie and her sister Rebecca come to Heather House to recover from the drowning deaths of their two husbands. But the house seems to be haunted by the ghost of its one-time owner, Heather Lambert, the scent of the eponymous herb occasionally drifting through the air. As Maggie falls under the spell of the house, events take a more sinister turn when she narrowly survives an attempt on her life, and then the housekeeper is found murdered ... Can Maggie discover the secret of Heather House before it's too late?

HANGOVER HILL

Mary Wickizer Burgess

A young woman goes missing while taking a summer job in an old mining town in California's scenic Sierra Mountains. Gail Brevard and her partners are called in to investigate the case, and she decides she must go undercover in order to get to the truth of the matter. A cruel arson murder followed by an explosion at an old mine threaten Gail's life, as she and her colleague try to put all the pieces of the puzzle together and prevent further tragedy . . .

TERROR STRIKES

Norman Firth

To Chief Inspector Sharkey, the first murder is baffling enough: on a nightclub dance floor, a man suddenly begins to choke. Horrified onlookers watch as he collapses and dies. It is quickly established that he has been strangled by someone standing directly behind him. But witnesses all testify that there was no one near him to do it. When this death is followed by a whole string of similar murders, Sharkey begins to seriously wonder if Scotland Yard is up against something supernatural . . .

THE JOCKEY

Gerald Verner

A man calling himself the Jockey begins a campaign against those who he believes have besmirched the good name of horse racing, escaping conviction through lack of evidence. In a message to the press, he vows that those who have amassed crooked fortunes will have the money taken from them, whilst those who have caused loss of life will find their own lives forfeit . . . When the murders begin, Superintendent Budd of Scotland Yard is charged to find and stop the mysterious avenger. But is the Jockey the actual murderer?